Liar, Liar

Ethan McWyer

Seek truth!!

Allie Slocum

Character Club Series

Liar, Liar Ethan McWyer

A Journey Toward Integrity

by Allie Slocum

Appeals to third through sixth graders.

Cover design by Todd Slocum, artwork by Kaylie Slocum, Beck's picture by Rylie Slocum.

ISBN: 9781981677887

www.characterclubonline.com

This book is
dedicated to my family:
Todd, Kaylie, & Rylie –
my biggest supporters
and *favorite people.*

Preface

Teachers, you may access the discussion questions included at the end of this book to help students respond in journals or in group discussions. For actual project ideas, visit

www.characterclubonline.com

These stories were birthed from the desire to instill strong character virtues in children. Allie started Character Club with thirteen girls when her oldest daughter was in third grade. It grew to eighteen students by the time her daughter was in fifth grade. Allie then started a coed club at her church. Now she is teaching the second generation of Character Club with her younger daughter's age group. She is forever looking for good stories that students can relate to with applicable lessons and activities. She hopes these books and website will inspire students *and* teachers.

Acknowledgments

I am so thankful for the "village" of people who helped make this book possible.

First and foremost, my Creator, author of all creativity. Thank you for the opportunity to share this story.

Todd Slocum, my ever-patient husband, who puts up with my endless ideas and "demands." Thank you for still wanting to be a part of all this. Kaylie and Rylie Slocum, our fun and creative daughters, the best listeners, mini cheerleaders and artists. Thank you for wanting to "work" for me.

Christy, my first "grade-school-mom-friend." Thank you for all your medical knowledge.

Mrs. William's 2016–2017 fifth grade classroom, especially the members of the focus group: Declan, Isaac, Jersey, Thomas, Tyler, Wes. Your ideas, input, and enthusiasm made this story worth sharing.

For all my beta readers–Jane, Nancy, Abby, Sharon, Sandy, Robin, Carrie, William, Winston, Laura, Hailey, Charli–thank you so much for your valuable input, advice, and edits.

Deb Hall, editor extraordinaire, so thankful to get to know you and work with you.

Contents

1 ~ So Long, Summer 1

2 ~ First Day Flub 13

3 ~ Shrewd Substitute 26

4 ~ Field Trip Follies 40

5 ~ Good Game? 57

6 ~ Triplet Trouble 76

7 ~ Character Club 95

8 ~ Dinner Date 115

9 ~ Facing Fear 129

Discussion Questions 144

Glossary 148

1 ~ So Long, Summer

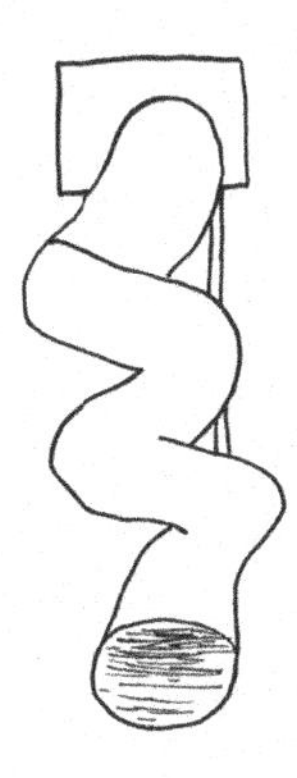

"Come on, Ethan! Race you to the bottom!" Harley called out as she catapulted herself through the giant blue tube.

Ethan McWyer sat at the top of the red waterslide in his bathing suit. His heart was racing faster than a freight train. These were the tallest twin slides at the neighborhood pool. Ethan had climbed two flights of stairs to get to this position. He listened to his younger sister's laughter and squeals as she rounded each curve inside the long tube. Down below, he watched

Harley finally shoot out the bottom of the slide. Her feet flew up in the air. She held her nose as her head went under. Ethan observed her emerge and adjust her suit. Ethan's legs tingled, just watching.

Harley looked around for her brother. When she couldn't find him, she looked up at the top of the slide where he still sat. Her face wore a frown.

Thank goodness the pool wasn't very crowded today, Ethan thought as he watched her dog-paddle to the side of the pool. Then she impatiently sat on the first step in the water. She put her elbows on her knees, her chin in her hands, and her bottom lip out. "Pout position" is what their dad called it.

Ethan was eleven years old and the soccer star of his team. He ran faster than anyone in his class. It seemed ridiculous to him that he couldn't make himself go down this slide. And yet, here he sat.

Ethan conquered the smaller slides long ago. The five-foot slide that was about his size caused no fear at all. He could even jump off the diving board into the deep end. But this slide felt taller than a skyscraper!

Ethan's six-year-old sister looked up at him shading her eyes with her wet hand. Two little, red pigtails dripped on either side of her head. Her pout faded and a look of determination came over her.

"Come on, Ethan. You can do it!" she called up to him.

"I'm coming!" he answered.

The last thing he needed was for her to call attention to him sitting at the top of the slide. Everyone would know he was too chicken to come down. He watched another boy start down the blue slide next to him.

Ethan's thoughts flashed back to the first time his dad took him to a professional basketball game. A friend had given Kolt, Ethan's older half brother, two tickets. Kolt was busy, so he passed them on to his dad and Ethan. It was so last minute that Ethan's dad never even looked at them until they were inside the arena.

The seats were in the very last row of the stadium, literally up against the wall at the top of the building. Ethan remembered how dizzy he felt walking higher and higher up the skinny cement staircase. Once they turned around and sat down, Ethan almost passed out. He clutched the arms of his seat so tightly his knuckles turned white. When his dad offered him some popcorn, he couldn't even get his hands loose to accept it. He never ate even one kernel.

Ethan was so distracted by his fear of heights that he couldn't enjoy any of the game either. He just wanted it to be over. He didn't even remember who the teams were or what the score was. He may as well not have been there. It was a good thing basketball was not his favorite sport.

Now he faced a new challenge. His little sister had dared him to go down the giant tube slide by the end of summer. Today was the very last day of summer. If he didn't go down the slide, he would be forced tomorrow to wear the shirt his ditzy Aunt Jane gave him. Tomorrow was the first day of school!

Aunt Jane was a very crafty woman, and she loved her niece and nephews. She was Ethan's dad's only sister. She was older and single with no children of her own. Aunt Jane always sent home-crafted items to Ethan and his siblings. This particular shirt displayed pictures of the whole family's heads bobbling on top of caricature-style bodies while balancing on the backs of dolphins.

Aunt Jane was very wealthy and enjoyed funding family vacations. She took them all to California earlier that summer to swim with dolphins. Ethan thought it was the only way she could get them to spend time with her. The shirts were parting gifts, which quickly became the subject of many family jokes.

Dares were serious business in the McWyer household. Not to follow through meant public humiliation every time. And usually it meant putting to use one of Aunt Jane's gifts. Aunt Jane always received a picture of the person in her gear and assumed it meant the family loved the gifts. This encouraged her to keep sending them.

Once, after Ethan's mom refused to dunk her head underwater at some hot springs, she had to wear the Christmas reindeer pajamas from Aunt Jane to work. Ethan thought it would have been better just to get her head wet, but his mother proudly drove off that morning in the reindeer jammies!

Ethan could possibly get away with blowing off a dare from Harley, but she had begged Kolt to "double-dog" dare him just this morning. Once two McWyers were involved, it was a lost battle.

Ethan sat frozen at the top of the slide trying to muster up the courage to force himself down. He watched Kolt saunter over to the diving area to get a better view.

Kolt was seventeen and in high school. He had a lot of friends but never seemed to mind taking Ethan and Harley places. Kolt was only two years old when his mother died. Ethan's mom once explained to Ethan that she died of a rare disease.

Ethan's parents met when Kolt was in preschool where Ethan's mom taught. Ethan wasn't even a thought in anyone's mind at that time. His mom was young, single, and new to teaching. Her name was Miss Adams. Kolt had struggled coming to school. He worried something would happen to his dad too. His dad could barely cope with getting him dressed in the morning. Miss Adams took Kolt under her wing. She and Kolt bonded in a unique way.

Mr. McWyer found himself spending a lot of time volunteering in Kolt's class that year to help Kolt's fears. Mr. McWyer seemed to want to bond with Miss Adams too. They began dating after a field trip to the zoo. Mr. McWyer proposed at the preschool graduation party. They became Mr. and Mrs. McWyer two months later. Their wedding boasted more four-year-old attendees than any other in history, so the story went. Ethan came along two years later. Kolt was a full brother in Ethan's mind, but Kolt kept his distance sometimes.

Today Kolt stood on the opposite side of the pool from Harley. Ethan was so thankful that John and Jack weren't here. John and Jack Cooke were identical twins who lived around the corner. The three of them usually hung out together all summer long. They were on the same soccer team. Most days after a game or practice they came to the pool to cool off.

Ethan managed to avoid the slide with the twins all summer by challenging them to constant games of pool basketball. The net in the pool sat just around the corner from the bottom of the slides. Thankfully, the twins never thought about the slides when they played basketball. Today, their mother took them shopping for back-to-school supplies, so Harley insisted Ethan make good on her dare.

Ethan was thinking it was now or never when suddenly he felt a huge force at his back.

"Dude! Get going! We're dying back here."

A mammoth kid, whom Ethan never even saw, gave him a huge shove. Ethan's eye struck the top of the tube as he was hurled down the slide. His body swished up around the side of each curve. He threw his arms out to try to keep from flipping over. His eye stung. He gasped and swallowed a mouthful of water. Finally, his body shot out of the bottom of the slide and his head quickly sank under the water. He flailed around for a second to get his bearings and stood himself up in the four-foot-deep water. He coughed and sputtered.

The mammoth kid who pushed him shot out of the tube almost immediately behind him. The boy's feet connected with Ethan's rear and knocked him back under the water.

Ethan's sister stood up on her step, stomped her foot, and yelled, "Hey!" Harley jumped from her spot onto the humongous boy, knocking him below the water as her knee connected with his jaw. Ethan resurfaced and turned to see Harley and the boy go under. Ethan looked down and saw a bit of red in the pool. He touched his eye. It stung. He pulled his hand away and saw it was covered with blood.

The lifeguard whistled. Ethan turned to look as Harley and the boy surfaced. She whistled again and forcefully motioned for them to get out of the pool. The lifeguard gathered them all around her about to give a speech. She took one look at Ethan's eye and instead sent all three of them to the pool office.

The manager sat down with the unlikely group. Another lifeguard handed Ethan some ice. Ethan placed it over his throbbing eye and attempted to look at his attacker with his other one. The giant, black-haired boy, an eighth grader nicknamed Brick, stared back at him.

He held an icepack near his mouth. A scar ran down his hand from his thumb to his wrist.

Harley sat with her arms crossed and a big pout on her face. Kolt leaned back against the doorpost waiting for them all to be thrown out.

"Do you mind explaining to me what just happened?" the manager questioned.

Harley was first to offer her side. "That nasty boy pushed my brother down the slide!" she yelled as she pointed her tiny finger in his face.

Brick countered, "What?! You jumped on me when I came out of the slide. Are you crazy?"

"You knocked him underwater at the bottom too!" Harley didn't back down. Ethan said nothing. Kolt stood there grinning, seemingly amused by the whole situation.

"He knows you're not supposed to wait at the bottom. You have to swim to the side right away," Brick argued back.

"And you know you are supposed to wait at the top till it's all clear. You did that on purpose!" Harley was standing directly in front of the boy's face with her hands on her hips. Ethan tried not to chuckle despite the pain and the cold by his eye. He knew arguing with Harley was a losing battle.

The manager impatiently stepped in. "Well, it looks like everyone broke some pool rules today. It's been a long summer. Call your parents to come pick you up. You're all outta here."

"I'm the small ones' ride," Kolt explained, pulling the car keys from his bag. "Come on, you two."

Harley spun around with her hands still on her hips ready to argue. Kolt stepped forward and scooped her up in his arms. Ethan resented being called a "small one," but he stood to follow Kolt. "Let's get you guys home." Kolt struggled as Harley kicked and punched him trying to get him to put her down. Ethan could see Kolt was also attempting to keep a straight face. He was completely amused by his little sister's antics. She, on the other hand, hated being humiliated.

Ethan followed behind the two of them and looked over at Brick who scowled after them. Catching his reflection in the office window as he passed by, Ethan was horrified. He could already tell he was going to have a black eye for the first day of school. How would he explain that to everyone? He could just imagine it. Uh, yeah, I was too afraid to go down the slide, so an eighth grader pushed me. I whacked my eye on the edge of the tube and screamed like a girl the whole way down. Then my little sister attacked the guy.

That was not going to happen. Ethan would rather wear his aunt's weird T-shirt.

2 ~ First Day Flub

"Wow! That had to hurt! What happened to your eye?" Darren exclaimed when he saw Ethan the next day at school. Darren Marks was an only child and a tall, tough fighter. He didn't talk much and was hard to impress. He seemed super fascinated with Ethan's black eye, though.

Ethan had tried to get out of going to school this morning. He complained to his mother how much his eye hurt when he woke up, even though it really didn't bother him that much. She calmly explained that a black eye couldn't keep him from the first day of school.

When skipping school hadn't worked, Ethan tried to wear his favorite black T-shirt, soccer shorts, and blue baseball hat hoping to hide his eye. But his mom would have none of that.

So Ethan dressed in a button-down, short-sleeve shirt that his mother insisted he wear. She was a stubborn redhead like Harley. The shirt was tucked neatly into the dark jeans his mom bought him the day before the pool incident. His light brown hair grew out long enough over the summer that it covered some of the bruise. Thank goodness getting pushed down the slide counted toward Harley's dare. He was freed from wearing Aunt Jane's embarrassing T-shirt.

The first day of school always caused a big production at Ethan's house. His mom cooked a full egg casserole, complete with fruit salad and cinnamon rolls. By the time breakfast ended, Ethan often felt like rolling himself to school. But first, the rest of his mom's traditions had to be followed. Pictures at breakfast. Pictures by the fireplace mantle. Pictures by the front door.

Ethan endured the first-day-of-school pictures on their front step with Harley. Harley posed, decked out in her perky little multicolored plaid dress with matching shoes and hair bows. She proudly displayed her "First Day of First Grade" sign.

Ethan was grateful his mom didn't make him display his grade sign anymore. Kolt was long gone when Ethan woke up. Ethan wondered if his mom made Kolt pose for first day of school pictures too. Ethan looked up to Kolt and always wanted to impress him. He wanted to impress Darren too.

Ethan suddenly heard himself say out loud to Darren, "Some kid was messing with my little sister at the pool yesterday. I told him to leave her alone and he swung. I never saw it coming. They kicked him out, on the spot."

"Wow." Darren was impressed. "Guys! Come check out Ethan's eye!"

A bunch of boys gathered around Ethan. Peter was one of them. He went to Character Club with Ethan after school on

Thursdays. Ethan retold his new story over and over. Each time he added a detail that made it sound a little better. By the third retelling, he even got a few swings in himself. Peter was super impressed and started following Ethan everywhere.

At lunch, Ethan was surrounded by more guys than ever before. Each one wanted him to repeat the story again and again. They would high-five or fist-bump each other when Ethan told the part about the kid getting kicked out. His best friends, John and Jack, sat at the end of the table both impressed and bewildered. Ethan wasn't the fighting type.

By the time Ethan got to science class, he was a hero. He sat down in the back of the room. Peter sat right next to him. Jeanie Blair, who also attended Character Club, walked in and sat down in front of Peter.

She looked right at Ethan and said, "That was super cool how you stuck up for your sister yesterday. I wish my little brothers were able to protect me."

Jeanie had three younger brothers who were triplets. Harley talked about them last year when they were in kindergarten together. One of them was a pretty good soccer player, but Ethan couldn't remember which one.

Jeanie turned away from him with a swish of her long brown ponytail when her best friend, Claire, bounded in. Claire skipped everywhere she went. Ethan loved the way her long blonde curls bounced along with her. He wished he could just stretch a curl out to see how it sprang back toward her head. Claire sat down right in front of him and listened to Jeanie retell Ethan's story. Her curls were so distracting that he almost missed Jeanie add the detail that the lifeguard had to pry Ethan and the eighth grader off each other. His story just kept getting better and better!

Then Mr. Sable, the science teacher, introduced himself to the class. He shared how excited he was to get to know each one of them. He explained that they would learn about ecosystems this year. Ethan zoned out replaying all the tellings of his adventure at the pool yesterday. He sensed a funny, nervous feeling in his stomach that maybe he did something wrong. But there was no way he could tell anyone that he had been the one attacked. How could he bear others knowing his sister was the tough guy and not him?

Ethan's attention snapped back to Mr. Sable's lecture when he heard the words "field trip." Mr. Sable now had Ethan's full attention.

"In just a few weeks we will be headed over to our state park to learn about all the ecosystems there. We can allow four parents to come, so if your parents are interested, have them return this form to me."

Mr. Sable started passing out forms. Jeanie got all excited as she turned to Claire and said, "My dad will come! He loves field trips."

Ethan knew his dad could never take off work to come, but his mom would be all over this. Sometimes she still went into teacher mode with his friends and it could get a little embarrassing. He could only imagine what she would be like on a field trip these days. It would be worse than being rescued by his little sister from a bully at the pool. Part of him was embarrassed for Jeanie. Didn't she know it wasn't cool anymore to have your parents on field trips?

After school he walked outside after the last bell rang with his new crowd of followers around him. He stopped suddenly when he saw the giant boy from the pool across the front lawn surrounded by his own group of guys. Brick was showing off his fat lip. It appeared his friends were just as impressed with Brick as Ethan's crowd was with him. I wonder if they know a six-year-old girl did that, he thought.

"Um." Ethan didn't want to wonder for too long. He tried to think quick. "I forgot something in my locker, guys. I'll see you tomorrow."

Ethan turned and ran back inside the school building. He ducked into the locker room and waited ten full minutes before attempting to walk home. When he emerged from the school a second time, there was no one in sight. He couldn't believe that kid went to his school. Of all the luck . . .

* * *

When Ethan finally sat safely around the dinner table that night, his mom asked how everyone's first day went. She served the one dish that the whole family ate and loved–beef burritos. Ethan dove right in.

Harley piped up with her monologue of the day. "Mrs. Dish is the prettiest teacher I ever saw! She has soft brown hair and wore a beautiful blue dress with apples on it. We are going to learn all about apples this month in science!"

Kolt interrupted, "How do you know her hair is soft?"

"She let me touch it during reading. She lets us give her back rubs too."

"Lets you?" Kolt raised one eyebrow.

"Yep!" Harley didn't skip a beat. "She read us a book about Johnny Appleseed. He planted apple orchards all across this whole country!"

Harley stood and panned her arm across the whole room imagining it was the wide-open country. "He wore a pot on his head and never wore shoes. He slept under the stars. He was a real mountain man. A snake bit him once and he almost died. But the Indians saved him. He was friends with everyone, even the animals!

He talked to them and they talked back! Can I get a bunny?"

Her dad chuckled as she turned to look at him. "Sounds amazing, Harley. We'll talk about bunnies next summer. Let's take a bite of your food and let one of your brothers share for a moment, okay?"

Ethan's dad never said no to anything. He just always deferred to summer. By the time summer came no one usually remembered what they wanted, so it didn't come up again.

Harley stuck out her bottom lip as she plopped back down in her chair. She picked up her fork knowing what her dad meant.

Ethan challenged Harley, "Are you sure Johnny Appleseed did all of those things?"

Harley nodded as she sat between their parents because she still tended to spill something at most meals. Harley wasn't exactly messy, but her stories could get very animated. Sometimes a cup just got in the way. She also needed a lot of reminders to stop talking and eat. Harley's mom rubbed her back to placate her.

Kolt took the floor. "There's a new girl

that I have several classes with. I think I might have seen her at the pool yesterday, but we got kicked out before I could even say hello." He gave a sideways look at Ethan and Harley.

"It wasn't our fault!" Harley stood up and stomped her foot. "That boy was a bully!"

"I would agree with that," their mom said, nodding. "I can't believe he pushed my boy down that slide." She turned to Ethan seated on her other side. She brushed Ethan's hair back to look at his eye.

"Mo-om." Ethan shook his head to let his hair fall back down.

Kolt continued in a half-mocking, half-joking tone. "Well, all I know is I was on the way over to introduce myself yesterday when a certain redheaded ball of fire got us thrown out of the pool by attacking a man-boy twice her size!"

"You don't have to go and rub it on me!" Harley plopped herself back down and crossed her arms. Her bottom lip protruded again.

The entire family burst out laughing. Seeing Harley's confused look, their mom explained, "It's rub it in, honey."

"Oh." Harley cracked a smile. She may have a temper, but it could be cured quickly with a laugh. And thankfully, she was willing to laugh at herself.

Ethan's dad got a hold on his laughter and turned to Ethan. "How about you, buckaroo? How was your day?"

"Yeah, buckaroo! How was it? Did everyone love the story of how your kid sister saved you from drowning yesterday?" Kolt playfully punched Ethan's arm as they sat side by side at the round table.

Ethan rolled his eyes. "Da-ad, I'm not five anymore. I'm not your buckaroo. It was fine."

"Don't roll your eyes at your father, Ethan," his mom said, pushing his hair back once again. "Did you bring any papers home for me to sign?"

Ethan's mom loved filling out school forms. She said it made her feel like she was still a part of teaching. Ethan's dad once explained that she seemed a little melancholy every August when they started getting ready for the back-to-school days.

"Of course, Mom. Tons. You'll have a blast. Plus, there's one for a field trip to the state park next month. I'll need some money for that," Ethan answered.

"A field trip! How exciting. Does your teacher need volunteers? I'd love to go." Ethan's mom wore a silly grin across her face.

"Um . . . no. He said it's just teachers this time." Ethan swallowed as he lied to his mother. He kept his eyes glued to his plate so as not to make eye contact with her.

"Oh. That's disappointing. I used to love field trips. Students act so differently. It was a chance to really get to know them personally," she reminisced.

"Not to mention a field trip was kind of our first date." Ethan's dad winked at his mom.

She blushed. "Of course. How could I ever forget that field trip? Changed my life."

Ethan watched them look at each other in that dreamy way that they still did sometimes. "Remember the leapfrogging kangaroos?" his dad snorted.

His mom almost spit out her water as

she laughed along with him. "I'd never seen anything like it!" Parents can get so weird and awkward at a moment's notice.

"Sorry," Ethan mumbled, interrupting their trip down memory lane. "I'm not actually feeling that well. May I be excused?"

His mother looked away from his dad and into his eyes. Ethan quickly looked down at his plate. His mom always said she could see it in his eyes when he was sick. She tucked his hair back one more time and said, "Sure, sweetie. First day can be exhausting. Why don't you go lie down in your room?"

Ethan got up slowly so it looked like he didn't feel good. Inside, he just wanted to race to his room as quickly as possible, although his stomach definitely didn't feel quite right. He forced himself to walk methodically through the kitchen and down the hall to his room. As he plodded along, he heard Harley say from the table, "I'll be your buckaroo, Daddy."

3 ~ Shrewd Substitute

A few weeks into the school year, Ethan tried to relax in his worry about Brick. Ethan's eye healed up, and the incident seemed mostly forgotten among the other boys. Ethan managed to avoid Brick in the halls and after school.

But as the weeks continued to go by, a nagging feeling that something wasn't right followed Ethan. He often felt like something was chasing him. He started to get jumpy seeing shadows or hearing things that weren't really there. It was beginning to be a real problem.

One Wednesday morning, he overslept while having a dream. In Ethan's dream he sat in the school cafeteria surrounded by his admirers. Darren, Peter, John, Jack, and other boys hung on every word he said. Claire and Jeanie perched at the end of the table batting giant eyelashes at him. Even Mr. Tom, the building manager, stood at the end of the table leaning on his broom, fully tuned in to Ethan's story.

Suddenly, Brick barreled into the cluster. He hurled baseball-sized chicken nuggets at Ethan's face. The girls scattered. Mr. Tom vanished. The other boys counterattacked with broccoli and carrots.

Ethan sat frozen in place. He couldn't run away or join the fight. His arms felt pinned to his sides. He tried to yell and gain control of his body as Brick drew closer. The towering boy climbed up over the table. Ethan's protectors were no match for this giant. Brick just kept coming as food bounced off him like little spit wads. He grabbed Ethan's arm and drew back to punch him. Ethan flailed in defense as he heard who he thought was Claire calling from the other side of the cafeteria.

Ethan finally began to awake to his mother's voice. "Ethan, are you sick?"

She stood over his bed shaking him. "Ow!" she exclaimed as Ethan, still flailing around in his dream, whacked her shoulder.

"Hey! You overslept. I just got back from dropping Harley off at martial arts practice before school. I expected to find you at the kitchen table eating breakfast. Get up quick. Are you okay?" She rubbed her shoulder where Ethan's fist connected with it.

Ethan jumped up. He looked back at his bed, half expecting Brick was crouched there ready to pounce. He observed nothing but a massive knot of sheets and blankets. Ethan shook himself off. He dressed quickly and headed downstairs.

Ethan's mom handed him a protein bar as he raced out the door with less than ten minutes until the bell rang. Ethan only lived four blocks from the school, but he liked to take his time. On normal days, Ethan usually met the twins at the corner to walk the rest of the way together. There was no sign of them today.

Ethan ripped open his protein bar as he rounded the corner from his street. No time for rock kicking today. No moments for picking a stick to drag along. This morning it would have to be a full-out sprint. He took giant bites as he ran along the main street that led to the school. He passed Mrs. Keller's street which turned off to the right.

Suddenly, he heard the warning bell ring. He tossed his wrapper and bolted for the school building. Ms. Warber did not tolerate tardiness at all. She taught reading and writing. Ethan spent his first class with her each morning.

Ethan skidded through the classroom door as the late bell rang. He looked over at Ms. Warber's desk and discovered a substitute teacher sitting in her place. She barely looked up at him as he hoofed it to his seat.

The boys always messed around whenever a substitute visited a classroom. It was almost a contest to see who could get away with the biggest prank. John and Jack always switched identities. They already sat at the other one's desk. Ethan could tell them apart from knowing them since their preschool days. Ethan's mom had to peek at the small mole by John's right ear to tell them apart.

This substitute met the class prepared and ready, though. She immediately marched to the front of the room and said, "I'm Mrs. Murray. The good news is I don't know you, but the bad news is I don't know you."

She paused to let her comment sink in. "I'll explain. If you have a reputation for messing around in class or not doing your work very well, I don't know that. So today is a fresh start for you. You could be the best student here!

"But if you are the teacher's pet, I don't know that either. So you'll have to earn my trust from the beginning. Today, everyone has a clean slate. So make good choices and we will all have a great day. Make bad choices and I can get really mean, really quick."

Ethan raised his eyebrows and looked over at Peter. Peter gave him a mischievous look. Tomas–a troublemaker on the playground but goody two-shoes around the teachers–looked panicked. Darren's face revealed nothing.

When Mrs. Murray turned her back to write her name on the board, John and Jack rubbed their hands together with sneaky looks in their eyes. A few girls whispered to each other. Eddie and Brad made faces and hand gestures back and forth mimicking the substitute's speech. Mrs. Murray, still facing away from the class, commented, "And I don't appreciate being mocked behind my back."

When Mrs. Murray faced them again, she looked right at Eddie. Eddie's eyes widened and he quickly grabbed a notebook. Brad, undeterred, popped a piece of chewing gum in his mouth. Mrs. Murray didn't miss it for a second. "Young man, does your teacher allow you to chew gum in class?"

Brad answered confidently, "Yep."

"That would be yes, ma'am. Please." Mrs. Murray wasn't convinced and turned to Ethan sitting directly across from Brad. "Is that true?"

Ethan looked up at her and then around at the other boys. He paused. Ms. Warber only let them have gum if they were taking a standardized test, but he couldn't let the boys down. "Yes, ma'am . . . as long as we keep it quiet." He was beginning to lose track of how many lies he'd told.

Mrs. Murray nodded and began the lesson. She turned to write the assignment on the board. Ethan watched Eddie, Peter, and Darren all pop a piece of gum in their mouths. Eddie gave him a thumbs-up. Wendy–another girl from Character Club–looked at him with wide eyes as she shook her head with disappointment. Ethan didn't feel much like celebrating or chewing gum. He felt that nagging feeling creeping up again.

Once the students appeared to be working independently, Tomas walked over and whispered something to Mrs. Murray who had sat down at Ms. Warber's desk. She looked over at Ethan as Tomas finished and her eyes narrowed. Ethan gulped. She didn't move or say anything, and Tomas went back to sit down.

About ten or fifteen minutes into class, a girl named Amanda went over to Ms. Warber's desk and asked, "Can I go to the bathroom?"

Mrs. Murray said, "I don't know, can you?"

Amanda restated her question, "May I go to the bathroom?"

Mrs. Murray nodded but then motioned Amanda closer and quietly asked her a question. Mrs. Murray nodded with understanding as Amanda answered, and glanced over at Ethan. Ethan quickly looked down at his book. He felt a nervous flutter in his chest.

Amanda grabbed the hall pass and left the room. Ethan noticed a few girls slipping notes to each other. He watched Eddie pull some slime out of his desk to play with while his folder stood up to block Mrs. Murray's view. Peter and Darren whispered as they passed fidget toys back and forth. The twins started folding paper into shapes. Ethan wasn't sure if they would be airplanes or some kind of origami.

As Ethan attempted to be the only one in the room actually doing his first assignment, he realized that he had rushed out the door without a morning visit to the bathroom. Suddenly, his full bladder had to be emptied . . .

now! He quietly walked over to the teacher's desk. Mrs. Murray was watching Peter and Darren whisper to each other. Just as he got there, she called out sternly, "You two boys, move to different tables." Then she looked at Ethan with a disapproving look. "Yes?"

"I need to use the restroom," Ethan explained.

"Does Ms. Warber let you use the restroom during class?"

Ethan began to nod, but she continued, "Never mind. You are the one who lied about the gum. I can't trust you now, especially to leave the classroom. Trust shattered is hard to rebuild. It takes a long time. You and I don't have it today. Go sit down."

"But..." Ethan wanted to explain how he overslept and rushed out the door. Mrs. Murray just circled her finger in the air indicating he needed to turn around and go sit down. The conversation was over. Ethan shuffled back to his seat. All he could think about now was needing to get to that restroom.

Amanda returned and Ethan realized she had been gone a long time. He watched as her friend Valerie stood up and asked to leave. Mrs. Murray let her go. Ethan felt the injustice of it all. He tried to concentrate on his work, but his bladder wouldn't let him. He watched the clock until Valerie finally came back in the room. She had been gone ten minutes!

He watched Valerie look at Amanda and wink. She then nodded at a girl named Maria. Ethan knew the three of them were best friends. He watched Maria stand up and go ask to use the restroom. He could tell Mrs. Murray was getting frustrated, but she still let Maria go. Ethan knew they were up to something. Only a girl would have any idea what, though.

Ethan thought his bladder was going to explode. He waited five more minutes, then stood again to ask to leave. Mrs. Murray saw him beginning to stand and just put her hand up and motioned for him to sit back down. Ethan plopped down in his desk. His leg started bouncing uncontrollably. He watched the clock. He wished he had just told the truth. Who cared what the guys thought when he needed to pee so badly. This felt like torture. Another seven minutes went by before Maria came back in. The three girls all smirked at each other before she sat down.

Ethan wondered if an eleven-year-old could have an accident. He felt his eyes watering. Was he going to pee out of his eyes? He looked at the clock again. Fourteen more minutes. He could make it fourteen more minutes, right? The second hand creeped along with agonizing indifference to Ethan's predicament. It shocked him how long that small lever took to get all the way from the twelve around the circle and back to the twelve again when he was watching it. That same little hand always flew around during soccer games. He fidgeted with his pencil.

A loud noise startled him from the back of the room. Valerie screamed, "A mouse!" Maria and Amanda screamed and jumped up on their chairs.

Then Amanda shouted as she pointed toward the bookshelf, "There it goes!"

Mrs. Murray bolted out of her chair to the corner where the girls pointed. Everyone rushed over to have a look. Ethan took the opportunity to race out of the classroom. As he scurried down the hall, he smiled to himself. He knew there was no mouse. Mr. Tom–the real building manager, not the one from his dream–prided himself on the fact that their school was pest-free. It surprised Ethan that the girls were the ones who enabled him to get out of class. He might need to thank them later. He'd never felt such relief.

* * *

That Thursday after school, Ethan walked to Character Club with John, Jack, Jeanie, and Claire. Most of the kids walked there in groups since Mrs. Keller's house was so close to school.

Mrs. Keller taught elementary school before she became a mom. She retired to raise her children but missed teaching, so she started the Character Club. Her children, Andrew and Karlie, were in high school now and assisted her with the club. Sometimes Karlie even dressed up in character to teach a lesson about a historical figure.

Claire and Jeanie strolled ahead listening

to John tell about the "mouse incident" from yesterday. Jack and Ethan followed several steps behind. Jack asked, "Do you ever worry that you'll run into that kid from the pool?"

"Nah," Ethan lied.

"I sure would," Jack confided. "I think I'd be looking around every corner expecting him to pop out and hit me again."

Ethan reeled back, surprised. Jack just read his very thoughts. Before he could comment, Ethan watched Jack stoop over and pick up some trash off the ground.

"Gross. Why are you doing that?" Ethan asked.

Jack shrugged. "Mrs. Keller must be rubbing off on me. Remember last spring when she taught us about responsibility and taking care of our community? Ever since then, I try to pick up trash in our neighborhood when I see it. If we, the people who live here, don't take care of it, who will?"

Ethan shrugged as Jack flipped over the wrapper. He realized it was from his protein bar yesterday. A nagging cringe rippled through his insides. Maybe he wasn't the most responsible kid in the club.

"Let's just hope 'pool guy' doesn't show up at Character Club!" Jack joked.

Ethan's face went white and his stomach dropped. He gulped, "Why would you say that?"

"Not worried about him, huh? Yeah, right," Jack guffawed.

4 ~ Field Trip Follies

A few weeks later, the day of the field trip finally came, which meant a day free of worry from bumping into Brick. Ever since his talk with Jack, Ethan felt even jumpier about running into Brick. Brick kept showing up in his dreams over and over. The best dream would instantly be wrecked with Brick popping out from behind something and attacking him.

In the latest one, Brick rang his doorbell dressed as a girl trying to sell him Girl Scout cookies. When Brick realized it was Ethan, he dropped the cookies and shoved Ethan backward. Ethan's living room turned into a giant slide that he fell down. He kept sliding, twisting and turning down and down forever, until he finally woke up.

Ethan found himself in Jeanie's dad's group for the tour. Mr. Blair was the only dad on the field trip, so he ended up with a lot of boys in his group. In addition to Jeanie, the only other girls were Claire, Amanda, Maria, and Valerie. Peter, Darren, Tomas, Brad, and Eddie were also in the group. There were also some boys Ethan never talked to. It was a group of fifteen in all.

Ethan overheard Mr. Sable whisper to Mr. Blair to keep a close eye on Darren and Tomas because they had just been in a fight at school a few weeks ago. Ethan remembered that day. It took place in the cafeteria. Darren and Tomas were a tangled mess pummeling each other. Ethan had gathered in the circle with the other boys watching until Mr. Tom broke it up.

Jeanie embellished a story about it that she accidentally shared with Tomas instead of her home computer. He forwarded it to their whole class the day he was home on suspension. Everyone seemed angry at Jeanie for that, especially Darren.

It turned out that Darren's mom had been in a terrible accident. Mr. Bostrick, their principal, helped Jeanie swallow a lot of pride and apologize. Ethan hoped that no one ever found out about his dramatized story about the black eye. It made Ethan feel better that he wasn't the only one who stretched the truth.

Ethan realized Mr. Sable gave Mr. Blair mostly troublemakers. Peter was the only other boy in the group who attended Character Club. But he was no role model for character. He threw a worm on a quiet, older girl named Rachel the same week Darren and Tomas got in the fight. Then Ethan started to wonder why he was in this group. Did Mr. Sable consider him a troublemaker?

On the bus ride to the park, the twins shared Ethan's seat and told jokes back and forth. Ethan stared out the window trying to think of a way to prove that he was not a troublemaker. He didn't know what could have put him on the "naughty list."

When they unloaded at the nature center, guides waited to lead them around the park. Ethan followed Jeanie, Mr. Blair, and the others in the group. Jeanie was bouncing with a level of excitement usually only seen from Claire. She grabbed her dad's hand and pulled him toward one of the guides. Ethan was almost embarrassed for her. He couldn't understand why she would want her dad along. That seemed so uncool.

It also seemed strange to see Darren getting along with Jeanie so well after what she did to him. Darren really seemed different since his mom's accident. Maybe Ethan would invite him to Character Club sometime.

The guide Jeanie chose was a little old man. Ethan thought he wouldn't even make it through the parking lot, not to mention all the nature paths. To his surprise, the guide shouted with enthusiasm when Mr. Blair's group approached.

"I was hoping this group would pick me! You look like a bright bunch! Let's get going!" With a wave of his hand, he took off at a pace that shocked Ethan. At first, the girls were running and doing cartwheels down the path. Jeanie and Claire flipped a few round-offs. But as the guide began to pull away, they focused on keeping up.

Ethan soon found himself hustling along as the group took an uphill path. It was a good thing he ran most days for soccer practice. Ethan was in good shape. Poor Peter, however, was not. He was huffing and puffing when their guide finally came to a stop at an overlook.

"My name is Mr. Mickle, and I love this park. It's been a state park for over forty years, but it's been around a lot longer than that! Just look at this view!"

Ethan's eyes scanned the valley they stood above. He could barely take in the dramatic red sandstone formations. He kept far back from the railing and didn't look down either. He hoped no one would notice his fear of heights. Ethan tried to distract his mind as he imagined which formations he could peg with the perfect, round rocks sitting at his feet.

His attention snapped back when he heard Mr. Mickle say the word "rattlesnake."

Claire heard the word too and was already panicking. "I'm so out of here. Get me back to the bus!"

She started to run, but Mr. Blair grabbed her arm and pulled her in. Jeanie was already hugging his other arm tightly. Claire was obviously comfortable there. Ethan figured she was almost part of the Blair family. He remembered Claire's mother suffered from a lot of health problems and wasn't even sure her dad was in the picture. Ethan thought the two girls would cut off poor Mr. Blair's circulation.

Tomas exclaimed, "Cool! Can we see one?"

Mr. Mickle calmly explained that the snakes were as afraid of them as some of them were afraid of the snakes. So the chances of seeing one were highly unlikely, but it was of absolute importance that everyone stay on the trail. He also explained that no one was allowed to wander off alone. With that comment, he gave Claire a warning look.

Claire grasped Mr. Blair's arm even

tighter. Jeanie and the other girls were nodding their heads like bobblehead dolls. It reminded Ethan of his Aunt Jane's crazy shirts. He imagined Claire's and Jeanie's heads coming out of rattlesnake bodies. He laughed out loud.

Mr. Mickle sternly pointed out that he was very serious. He then lightened his mood and said that this was a great spot for a few photos. A bunch of boys pulled out cell phones and snapped some pictures. Jeanie gave her dad a look, and he pulled out his phone to take a picture of Claire and her. They put their arms around each other and posed with big smiles. Amanda, Maria, and Valerie argued over whose phone they would use for a selfie. Mr. Mickle offered to take it for them, but they refused.

Ethan didn't have a phone and didn't see a need for one. Those three girls looked like total dorks, more interested in what they looked like than in the scenery around them.

Mr. Mickle went on to explain that the park boasted one hundred forty-five species of birds and over fifty species of butterflies. The thought of gentle, fluttering butterflies seemed to help the girls forget about rattlesnakes. He continued, "Up around the next corner, we'll have a great chance of viewing some of these. So keep your eyes open."

Ethan listened to Mr. Mickle describe the ecosystem they were standing on. "We call it 'disturbed' because men have constructed these unnatural guardrails and concrete pathways. These sections then create their own ecosystem." Mr. Mickle put his arms out wide and spun around to continue, "Imagine all of this area, two hundred years ago, as just wide-open space. No visitor center. No rails. No walkways..."

"No bathrooms," interjected Tomas. The boys all started laughing.

"There wasn't a need, young man. There wasn't a need. There were no people here then."

Mr. Mickle led the group back down the path from the overlook. As they worked their way around the park, he pointed out areas where animals came to feast. Around one tree, thousands of tiny acorn tops lay scattered. Mr. Mickle explained that this was a popular spot for the bears, deer, and elk to eat. "But not at the same time."

"That was the understatement of the year," Tomas commented in the back. Whether Mr. Mickle chose to ignore Tomas or just didn't hear him, Ethan wasn't sure. But Mr. Mickle just continued explaining about the woodlands, prairies, forests of ponderosa pine, and other ecosystems of the park.

Ethan wondered if Mr. Mickle was as tired of Tomas as most of the teachers at school were tired of him. Ethan sure was tired of him. Ethan seemed to always have classes with Tomas. He remembered Tomas throwing blocks at him all the way back in kindergarten.

Mr. Mickle finished explaining about the history of the park as the group circled around to the visitor center. Mr. Sable's group was already back and had unloaded the lunches from the bus. Ethan grabbed his and followed the rest of the group to a spot shaded by some shrubs and trees. Ethan sat by Eddie. They chatted back and forth between bites. Other groups collected in the eating area.

When the time came close to load up the buses and head back to school, most of Ethan's group members were in the bathrooms. Ethan sat alone finishing his chips, lost in thought over this weekend's upcoming soccer game. The team they would play was one of their toughest competitors. He imagined himself stealing the ball from their fastest player and scoring the tie-breaking goal. The crowd would go wild.

Suddenly, Ethan heard movement in the bushes behind him. He pictured Brick jumping out and tackling him to the ground. Ethan jumped up and yelled, startling himself and everyone near him. He turned to glimpse a member of one of the one hundred forty-five bird species fly out of the bush and into a nearby tree.

"What was it?" Jeanie asked in alarm. The boys from his group came running out of the bathroom area, each one yelling a different question.

"A snake?" Claire shrieked. Mr. Sable started heading across the picnic area toward the ruckus.

"Uh . . . yeah." Ethan jumped away from the bush adding a dramatic flare. "Yeah, there was a rattlesnake right there!" He pointed at the bush.

The attention of another group's tour guide turned toward Ethan. She jumped into safety mode. "Okay, boys and girls, let's clear this area." She came and stood between Ethan and the bush. "I think your group is about ready to head back to school anyway."

Mr. Sable agreed and started herding the students toward the bus. Peter, Eddie, Brad, and Darren all gathered around Ethan peppering him with questions and comments.

"A real rattlesnake!"

"Did you see its fangs?"

"How big was it?"

"Which way did it go?"

"Okay, boys." The tour guide interrupted. "Take your conversation to the bus." She waved her arms in broad circles to push them along.

The boys all climbed on the bus and took their seats. Peter tried to sit with Ethan to get information about the snake. Mr. Blair asked if he could sit with Ethan, so Peter moved over with Eddie. Ethan moved over to the window and gave a weak smile to Mr. Blair. The nagging feeling that was becoming too familiar crept up his throat.

Mr. Blair didn't say anything until the bus started moving. The first few miles were over gravel terrain and very loud and bumpy. As the bus bumped along, Mr. Blair quietly leaned over and whispered, "That snake looked an awful lot like a bird to me, Ethan."

Ethan looked up at him and blinked hard. It was one thing to fool a bunch of fellow classmates, but here was an adult calling him out. His stomach did that flip-floppy thing it did every time he remembered the pool incident.

Mr. Blair didn't even give Ethan a chance to say anything. He started to tell a story instead. "When I was a bit older than you, my parents needed me to take my kid brother out with my friends one night. I didn't want to be seen with him, so I tried to ditch him all night. It was no use. We were at a bowling alley and there wasn't really anywhere to hide.

"As we were finishing up our pizza, one of the guys asked, 'Has anybody ever stolen anything?' I remember being surprised by the question and then shocked as each of the boys said yes. I had never stolen anything in my life. I knew it was wrong to take something that didn't belong to me.

"But suddenly all eyes were on me, including my kid brother's. I had to decide if I was going to lie to impress my friends or tell the truth to set an example for my kid brother. I remembered my dad's words when he would say, 'When you lie to others, you end up lying to yourself.'

"I looked over at my little brother and realized the kind of big brother I wanted to be. Even though I'd been angry earlier, I didn't want to be a liar. Or a thief. I told those boys that I never stole anything and I had no intention of ever doing it in the future."

Ethan asked, "What did the other boys do?"

"Well, a few of them said I was a coward and walked off. But one boy, Billy, said after they left, 'Wow. I wish I had the guts to have said that. I never stole anything either but didn't want them to think I wasn't cool. You're one brave dude.'

"It was a defining moment. I chose to be an honest person that day. Those three boys never talked to me again, but I'm thankful for it. One of them caused all sorts of trouble in the beginning of high school but moved away in the middle of the year. The other two stole on a regular basis and are both in jail for armed robbery.

"My mom once said honesty is its own reward. The look in my brother's eye, as Billy complimented me, was definitely worth it. Billy became my best friend and is to this day. I believe you know his twin sons."

"Mr. Cooke is your best friend?" Ethan was surprised. He didn't really talk to Mr. Cooke much. Mr. Cooke kept to himself most of the time.

Mr. Blair nodded and smiled. Ethan turned Mr. Blair's words over in his mind. He didn't think he had the guts to come clean with his story.

Back at school, Ethan sat trying to remember the names of all the ecosystems they'd seen for his journal assignment when Mrs. Murray walked in. Mr. Sable looked up at her and smiled. "Hey there."

Ethan wondered why she strolled in. Mr. Sable didn't look sick or like he was planning to leave for the afternoon. Ethan crouched down behind his computer to hide.

"Class," Mr. Sable interrupted their journaling. "Some of you have already had the pleasure of meeting my sister, Mrs. Murray. I helped her get a job subbing in our school. I'm sure you'll all be wonderful to her when she works with you in the future."

Well, that explains how I got on the "naughty list," Ethan thought. Mrs. Murray probably told her brother about her day with Ethan's class. She said in her own words she didn't trust Ethan at all.

* * *

The next day, Ethan went on another field trip with Character Club. Mrs. Keller was big on service projects. Every month the students did something in the community to give back or say thank you. Today, they were taking care packages to the local police department and getting a tour.

Mr. Blair was one of the volunteer parent drivers for the trip to the police station, as was Ethan's mother. She and Mrs. Keller used to teach together and stayed in close contact. Ethan thought they went to coffee at least once a month. He wasn't getting this field trip past his mother.

The police station proved exciting. Two officers led the group through the entire station. When the officers took them outside to see the patrol cars, the boys went wild. They began pummeling the officers with questions.

"Can we hear the siren?"

"Can you show us the lights?"

"Where do the bad guys sit?"

"Is it bulletproof?"

"How fast does it go?"

"Can we ride in it?"

The officers just laughed and patiently answered every question. Mrs. Keller kept reminding everyone to respectfully wait their turn. But in the end she just gave up and laughed with the police officers.

Ethan was slightly disappointed that he

couldn't actually sit in the car, but he understood that they were a big group. While waiting to load the cars and head home, Wendy, Jeanie, and Claire took turns flipping cartwheels in the grass outside the station. Ethan saw Mr. Blair and his mom talking. His mom looked over at him with a sad look in her eye. Uh oh, he thought, this can't be good.

5 ~ Good Game?

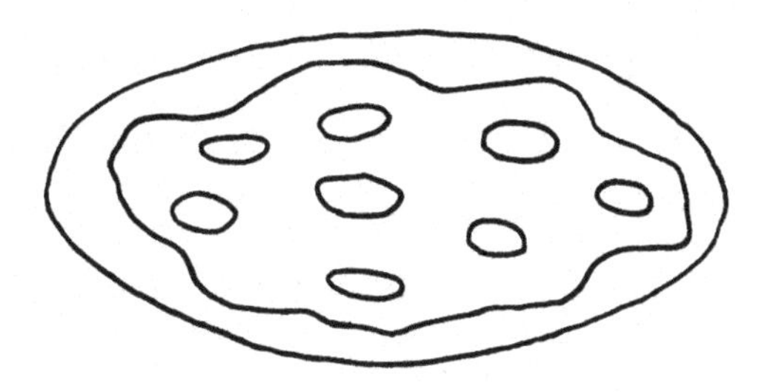

After she dropped the other kids off at Mrs. Keller's house, Ethan's mom didn't get out of the car to chat with Mrs. Keller like usual. Ethan didn't have a choice but to stay in the backseat where he had just ridden with Peter and a few other boys. She drove off down the street in silence. When they pulled up in front of their home, she turned the car off and quietly sat still for a second.

Ethan reached for the door handle, but she said, "Wait." Ethan dropped his hand to his lap.

"Mr. Blair told me how much he enjoyed having you in his group on the field trip yesterday." She paused to see if anything was sinking in. Her eyes connected with his in the rearview mirror. "I thought parents weren't allowed to go on that field trip."

Ethan realized he'd been caught. He sighed. The look on his mother's face made him feel like he had just ripped her heart out. "I'm sorry, Mom. I didn't think it would be cool for you to go."

She kept eye contact and said, "I just don't know which hurts worse, Ethan. That you didn't want me to go or that you lied to make sure I wouldn't."

She pulled herself out of the car. Ethan realized for the first time that his lying would catch up to him. There was definitely no reward in that.

Ethan's mom took Harley out for dinner that night and left Ethan alone with his dad and Kolt. Kolt stared him down like a criminal. "I can't believe you lied to Mom like that." Kolt was so protective of their mom, it made Ethan feel worse. He wanted to impress Kolt, not tick him off. It seemed like Kolt was against him lately. It was easier when they were younger, before Kolt went to high school. Now that he was a junior, Ethan felt like he annoyed Kolt more and more.

His dad actually stood up for him. "Kolt, Ethan needs to process this and figure it out on his own. I'll tell you one thing, son. A lie never leaves you alone. It follows you and grows larger and larger until it controls you. You become a prisoner to it. You constantly have to protect it and build on it. The only way to freedom is to confess or get caught. Neither one feels very good in the moment. But one ends a lot better than the other. And the longer the lie goes on, the more exhausting it is to keep it going."

Ethan thought about that. He actually did feel as if the walls were closing in around him every time he walked into the school building. But there was still no way he was going to tell everybody his kid sister defended him.

The next night at the soccer game,

Ethan couldn't concentrate. His mom sat in the crowd with Harley. His dad went to Kolt's game. Ethan wanted to shine on the field tonight to make up for letting his mom down. But everything he tried went wrong. He tried to pass to John and an opponent blocked it. He tried to head a ball and it went the opposite direction, causing another turnover. The worst was actually kicking the ball the wrong direction. Coach pulled him out for that one.

As Ethan sat on the bench, he watched Mr. Blair and all three of his triplets come sit by his mother in the bleachers. Jeanie wasn't with them. He wondered what he was going to get in trouble for this time.

When the whistle blew to end the game, Coach was not happy. They lost 4–2. He grumbled at the boys, "Meet me here tomorrow morning for an extra practice at eight o'clock sharp."

Ethan groaned with the other boys and slouched as he walked over to meet his mom and Harley. The Blair boys were nowhere to be found, but his mother wore a big smile on her face. "You'll get 'em next time, buckaroo." She ruffled his hair.

Ethan's face reddened as the sun's light faded behind the mountains. "Seriously, Mom. How can you be smiling right now? Or calling me buckaroo? This is ridiculous." His eyes darted behind him to see if any of the other boys from the team heard her comment. Thankfully, it didn't appear that any of them had. They were all wallowing in the loss as well.

"Hmm, it just so happens that Benjamin Blair is a big fan of yours. His dad just asked if you'd be willing to work with him on his game. And if you're willing to coach all three boys, he'll pay you."

Ethan's whole mood changed as his thoughts ran wild. Pay me? For playing soccer with a bunch of little boys? That sounded amazing.

He said, "Yeah, I'm willing! When do I start?"

"After you babysit Harley for me tomorrow night. Actually I don't have the details worked out yet. I figure if you are responsible enough to be in charge of three boys, you can watch Harley for Dad and me while we go out with Aunt Jane. She's coming to visit tomorrow."

Ethan rolled his eyes. Another Aunt Jane visit. He wondered what she would bring this time.

"But what about Kolt?" Ethan asked. He'd stayed home alone before, but never when Harley was there too.

"Kolt has a date with that girl he keeps talking about," his mom explained. "I figured you don't need to be going out with any of your friends after the not-so-lovely little lie you told me about the field trip."

"Oh." Ethan realized there was no point in arguing about that.

* * *

Ethan's mom worked it out that he could coach the triplets on Mondays after school. Their school included kindergarten through eighth grade. The plan was Ethan would meet them on the first grade playground for thirty minutes and then Mr. Blair would pick them all up.

Unfortunately, he would have to endure a punishing practice on Saturday before he started "working." Coach Capper did not seem any happier than he had the night before. His team windbreaker was zipped all the way up to his neck, and his hat was low on his head. The brisk autumn air revealed his angry breath. There wasn't so much as a "Good Morning" when they gathered.

Coach held his coffee cup tightly and sneered, "To the end of the field and back . . . twenty-five times."

The team inwardly groaned but silently complied. When the boys finished, they stood gasping for breath with their hands on their knees. Coach Capper explained his new plan of action. He taught them a move to draw an offside call from the referee. This would in turn earn the team an offside kick. The boys practiced the play for the rest of the hour.

Later that afternoon at their game, Coach Capper's plan worked. Their team was awarded the ball over and over and won 3–1! The team cheered and hollered in celebration. Ethan sprinted to the sidelines where his mom and Kolt waited. Kolt wore an irritated look on his face.

"Good game, buck– . . . I mean, buddy!" his mom congratulated.

"Thanks." Ethan was still breathing hard from playing the entire last period. He had definitely picked up the play more easily than any of his other teammates.

Kolt folded his arms across his chest and looked down at Ethan. "What was up with drawing the offside call so often? That almost looked intentional."

Ethan was startled by Kolt's reaction. "It was. Coach Capper taught us this morning. I'm the best at it. And we won!"

"Yeah, by playing slick and ticking the other team off," Kolt snorted. "I'm not impressed. Seems dishonest to me." He stalked off to wait for them in the car.

Ethan's mom watched him walk away, then turned back to Ethan and asked, "How do you feel about that?"

Ethan didn't know what he thought. First, Mr. Sable put him in the "difficult" group. Then his mom got so upset the other night about the field trip lie. Now Kolt was mad about his soccer game. No one seemed to be very happy with him.

Nobody, that is, except Jeanie Blair. She came rushing over from her brothers' game when it ended.

"I can't believe you are going to coach my little brothers! That's so cool, Ethan. You are the nicest guy to volunteer your time like that! Just watch for rattlesnakes in the field!"

Volunteer? Ethan wondered if he should tell her he was getting paid, but she turned and ran off as quickly as she came. Girls sure were confusing. It took a minute for Ethan to figure out her rattlesnake comment. Then he remembered the field trip. His lies were getting hard to keep track of!

John and Jack ran over to him after Jeanie left. "A bunch of us are going to the mall arcade tonight. Want to come?"

Ethan turned to look at his mom, but she was chatting with Coach Capper's wife. "Sure. When?"

"Six thirty," John explained.

"Perfect. See you there."

When they arrived at home, Dad and Harley were already back from her Saturday swim lessons. Aunt Jane and Harley sat on the couch chatting.

"Ethan! Kolt!" Harley called excitedly as she jumped off the couch. "I learned the butterfly stroke today! I feel like a frog when I do it, but I'm good at it! Want to see?" She threw herself down on the carpet and started the butterfly stroke. She looked ridiculous.

"You do look like a frog but good job." Ethan smiled at her. He walked into Aunt Jane's extended arms for one of her big bear hugs. Kolt also gave her a hug, then sat in a nearby chair.

"Oh, Ethan! You've grown so much! Now tell me, why did you have a black eye in your first-day-of-school picture?"

Ethan sighed and began, "I got into a fight with a boy at the pool the day before school started."

"No, you didn't!" Harley interrupted. "He pushed you into the slide and I jumped on him!"

Ethan turned to her and blinked a few

times. He told the other story so many times, he suddenly realized he had started believing it. "Oh, right." Ethan scratched his head. He glanced at Kolt who was shaking his head with a slight frown on his face.

Aunt Jane wasn't fazed. "Well, I was sorry to see that picture, no matter how it happened, so I bought you this to cheer you up. I actually brought one for everyone." Aunt Jane pulled six red clown noses out and lined them up on the coffee table.

Ethan's parents entered the room and stood behind the couch. Ethan stared at the clown noses. "I don't get it."

He looked up beyond his Aunt Jane to see his dad's reaction. His dad motioned with his hand sending the message to stop talking and just roll with it.

Ethan reached down and picked up a nose. He put it on and said in a nasal voice, "Thank you."

Aunt Jane smiled her giant toothy smile. "Let's all wear one for a selfie!" She passed the others out and the whole family adjusted their noses. Aunt Jane pulled out her phone and gathered the group together.

It was a tight fit until she exclaimed, "Oh! I'm so glad I brought my new selfie stick. Such a great invention. James, have you seen these?" Aunt Jane asked her brother.

"Nope. Maybe you can get me one." Ethan's dad laughed.

"Oh, not necessary. I'll just leave this one for you!" She clicked the button on the stick and captured the picture.

Ethan's mom complained as the image displayed on the screen. "Oh, I look just awful!" she squealed nasally.

"You look pretty, Mommy!" Harley argued.

"More like you have a bad cold," their dad laughed. He pulled off his nose. "We should get going, ladies."

Harley exclaimed, "I'b gonna leab my nose on awl night!"

"That will make it hard to have a conversation!" Kolt gave his aunt a hug and finished, "Sorry, but I need to head out too. It was good to see you, Aunt Jane. Thank you for the nose. I'm going to wear it to pick up my girlfriend."

Aunt Jane laughed, "Send me a picture!"

Kolt promised he would and headed out the door.

"Why cam't we cub witt you, Daddy?" Harley pouted.

Ethan's dad scooped Harley up and pulled off her nose. "Tonight your Aunt Jane, Mom, and I have some important matters to discuss. You would be bored out of your mind. You'll have a much better time playing with your brother." He set her down.

That was all Harley needed. She changed her tune and exclaimed to Ethan, "I can't wait to play with just you tonight! I have ten games picked out for us. There's Candyland and Go Fish. Then, Old Maid..."

Harley's voice droned on. Ethan realized he couldn't go out with the guys if he was babysitting Harley. He had totally forgotten. He tried to work out a plan in his head so he could do both. He felt like Mr. Blair dragging his kid brother to the bowling alley. He didn't want to do that.

His mom's phone rang. He heard her

answer then say, "Ethan, it's for you."

Ethan took the phone from her and heard John's voice. "So we decided to meet at the sporting goods store."

Ethan quickly walked out of the room so his family wouldn't hear him. "I can't make it after all, guys. Kolt wants to hang out just us brothers tonight." Ethan surprised himself to hear those words come out of his mouth. But it was what he really wanted to do.

"No worries. See you Monday," John said before hanging up.

Ethan went back into the kitchen as their mom started explaining, "Now tell Ethan to take the pizza out when the timer rings. Oh, Ethan, you're back. Great. So turn the oven off and let the pizza cool for about five minutes before you cut it to eat." Then she headed out the door. Ethan just nodded.

As soon as the door shut behind them, Harley turned and said, "Let's play! You shuffle."

Ethan did not love Candyland, but he shuffled the colored cards anyway. He arranged them so all the special cards were in order and near the top of the draw pile. He also made sure Harley would pick each of them. They blew through the game in less than ten minutes.

"That was the best game ever!" Harley exclaimed, not realizing Ethan's deception. "Let's do Go Fish next."

"I have a better idea," Ethan answered. "Let's play Road Crosser."

"That's a video game. I'm not allowed to play that without Mom and Dad."

"Yeah, but I'm here and I say it's okay." Ethan walked downstairs to the basement where the game center was kept. Harley followed.

"I don't know, Ethan." Harley put her hands on her hips and shook her head.

"Here. You can go first." He handed her the controller. Once Harley started playing, it was easy for them both to get caught up in the game. Each played two turns before switching. They went back and forth in this manner several times. One time, Ethan's character fell in a pothole just as he started.

"My turn!" Harley went to grab the controller.

"Just one more," Ethan argued.

Harley crossed her arms and her pout came out, but she watched him play again. When his character fell again, he quickly reset it hoping she wouldn't notice. He was so close to his best score!

"Hey! You said once more. That was two!" Harley did not miss this attempt to trick her.

"Fine. Here you go." Ethan went to hand her the controller and then sniffed. "What's that smell?"

"Oh no! The pizza!" Harley screamed and threw the controller.

The two of them raced up the stairs to the kitchen. Smoke poured out of the oven. Ethan pulled the door open and looked at the charred pizza. He grabbed a towel to pull it out, which did not work as well as a hot pad. When he grabbed it, the metal cookie sheet burned his hands. He yanked his hands back, which catapulted the pizza across the room. The pizza knocked a glass off the counter that shattered as it hit the floor.

"You did it now!" Harley scolded.

"Quiet," Ethan scoffed. "Just help me clean it up." Ethan opened a window to clear the smoke before the alarm would sound and began picking up the pizza pieces with a thicker towel.

He dumped them in the trash can while Harley picked up a piece of glass.

"Ouch!" Harley squealed and dropped it. A stream of blood ran down her finger. "Ethan! Help!" She held up her hand to show him and started crying hysterically.

"Oh boy. Let's get a Band-Aid." Ethan stepped around the pizza on the floor to grab her hand. He held the pizza towel tightly to her finger to stop the bleeding. The two of them tiptoed around the glass to get to the bathroom where their mom kept the Band-Aids.

Harley sat on the edge of the tub and cried, "I want Mommy!"

Ethan looked at her. "I'm sorry, Harley. I wish she were here too." Ethan found the biggest Band-Aid in the princess box and wrapped it around her cut. He was thankful the gash wasn't as big as he expected it to be.

Ethan wondered how he could calm

Harley down without calling his parents to come home. "I know! Let's have ice cream for dinner!"

Harley paused her crying to ask, "Really?"

"Yeah! Come on." Ethan took her good hand and led her back to the kitchen table. He sat her down, then carefully tiptoed around the mess to scoop up a big bowl of peppermint ice cream. Harley loved it because it was pink.

Once she was happily eating, Ethan found some rubber gloves under the sink to protect his fingers from being cut. He cleaned up the rest of the pizza and glass.

When the kitchen looked normal again, he scooped himself some chocolate ice cream and sat down with Harley. This was one time Ethan was glad Harley ate so slowly. "Let's not tell Mom and Dad about all this, okay?"

Harley studied Ethan's face. "Why not?"

Ethan studied her back. "Let's make it our special secret . . . ice cream for dinner!" He thought if she could focus on that, maybe she would forget the rest.

"Okay!" Harley smiled. "Deal!" She

held out her spoon to his and they clinked them.

After Ethan got Harley to bed, he went back down to the basement and picked up the controller from where Harley threw it. He played until he finally felt his eyelids drooping. He put everything away and climbed the stairs to his bedroom. Neither Kolt nor his parents were home yet. Ethan collapsed into bed.

6 ~ Triplet Trouble

On Sunday, nobody confronted Ethan or noticed any traces of the pizza disaster. Ethan's parents spent a lot of time talking in his dad's home office, though. Aunt Jane called several times but never insisted on talking to the kids like she usually did. Kolt took Ethan and Harley to the park but didn't pay a lot of attention to them.

Kolt kept checking his phone, texting now and then. Harley didn't seem to notice, but Ethan wondered what was going on. His parents hardly interacted with any of them the whole day.

On Monday in science class, Ethan gathered more attention than he liked. Jack approached him and scowled, "We saw Kolt at the mall Saturday night."

John added, "You weren't with him. Some girl was."

Ethan gulped. Before he could reply, Jeanie ran over with Claire and gushed, "I told Claire you are going to coach my little brothers! She thinks it's so cool too! Maybe she and I can come watch you sometime! You are just the nicest..."

Jeanie's voice motored on as Ethan decided he better tell her he was getting paid. His lies were definitely piling up. It was exhausting, like his dad had warned. But Mr. Sable settled everyone down and started his lesson. Ethan didn't get to talk to her again all day and forgot about it. He was more concerned with his best friends' anger.

After school, he met up with the triplets on the first grade playground, which held an old soccer field. The nets were long gone but the posts were still there. The boys whooped, hollered, and jumped with great excitement as they ran onto the field kicking their soccer balls. Beck gave Ethan a picture and announced, "For you. It's you and me. I drew it myself."

Ethan quickly realized he needed to burn off some of their energy. He sent them dribbling each ball down to the goal and back five times before they finally slowed down enough to listen. Ethan could tell that Ben was the best already. He outran his brothers and remained in control of the ball the whole time. Beck and Barton–although he couldn't keep track of which was which–alternated between chasing the ball and chasing bugs.

Ethan ran the boys through a few simple passing drills he remembered from when he was just getting started in soccer. Then he lined them up to take shots at the goal. Ethan stood behind the posts and started to retrieve the balls for the boys. After just a few shots from Beck and Barton, Ethan decided they needed to take turns chasing the balls themselves. The half hour passed quickly, and before he knew it, Mr. Blair was pulling up in his green Jeep

Grand Cherokee outside the playground fence.

"Dad! Watch this!" Ben exclaimed as his dad climbed out of the car. Ben dribbled the ball around his brothers and then drilled a quick shot at Ethan. Ethan stuck out his foot and stopped it with ease.

"Wow, Ben. That was great." His dad walked through the gate. A black and white Cavachon puppy came tearing across the field toward a ball. Beck and Barton ran straight for the dog.

They called together, "Henry!" and fell down on the field to let the little dog jump all over them. He licked their faces, sniffed the grass, and barked happy barks. Beck gathered their furry friend in his arms. Mr. Blair and Barton followed closely. Little Henry wiggled around so much that Beck finally put him down.

Ben kept his focus on Ethan. "Watch this." Ben started doing toe touches from one foot to the other.

Ethan encouraged Ben, "Great job!"

All of a sudden, Henry pounced on the soccer ball. He rolled right over it and did a somersault.

Ethan laughed. "That's a funny dog!"

Ben explained, "He's really Jeanie's, but we get to play with him sometimes too."

Mr. Blair added, "Poor guy was cooped up inside all day while Mom worked and I was away at meetings. I thought he would like a little exercise."

Ethan watched the little dog tear around the field while the triplets chased him. "He sure seems to be enjoying it!" Ethan laughed. He and Mr. Blair watched as the boys and puppy all ran around.

Then Mr. Blair interrupted the silence. "Thanks so much for your time today, Ethan."

Mr. Blair handed Ethan a twenty-dollar bill. Ethan's eyes widened at the prospects of what he could do with this money. He couldn't wait until next week to do it again. It hadn't felt like work at all!

Ethan thanked Mr. Blair. Then all the Blair boys, including the little dog, piled into Mr. Blair's Jeep and rode away.

Ethan dribbled his soccer ball all the way home. He tried to invent new drills that he could teach the triplets as he kicked the ball down the road. His attention then turned toward brainstorming ideas of what to purchase with his money.

When he arrived home, his celebrations were cut short. He walked in to find his mom sitting by Harley who was lying on the couch.

His mother looked at him through angry eyes. "What's this about Harley getting cut with glass?"

Ethan looked from his mother to Harley. Harley didn't look right. Her face was pale and she kind of stared right through him. "Um..." Ethan wasn't sure how to start. "I put a Band-Aid on it for her."

"Did you wash it?" his mother asked.

"Uh..." Ethan tried to remember. The night was kind of a blur.

"Ethan. Look at me." His mother's tone was sharp. Ethan met her stare. "The school called me today. Harley's finger was bright red and swollen. Her fever was over 102 degrees. She has a serious infection. Why would you not tell me she cut herself on glass? I've spent most of the day at the hospital. She's finally on antibiotics and going to be okay, but this is serious. If the school didn't catch it when they did, she could have died."

Ethan stood stunned while his mother's words sunk in. He looked at his sister lying there so limp. "I'm . . . so sorry."

Ethan watched the tears roll down his mother's cheeks. "And I can't believe you told her not to tell us! It's hard enough to deal with you lying to me, but when you trick your little sister into lying too . . . That's unacceptable, Ethan."

"Mom, I'm sorry. What can I do to help make up for it?" Ethan asked. He truly felt humbled and horrible for hurting Harley.

"We'll start with no electronics or screen time for a few weeks. You can focus that time on taking responsibility for things around here. No hanging with friends after school or on weekends until further notice."

"What about coaching the triplets . . . and Character Club?" Ethan asked fearfully.

"I guess you'll need to take a break from those too. You need to learn some responsibility and honesty first."

Ethan was horrified. He hadn't tried to hurt Harley. He looked into her sad eyes. Even now it looked like she was trying to comfort him.

"Actually, maybe you should still go to Character Club," his mom continued, changing her mind. "Maybe Mrs. Keller can reach you in ways that I can't seem to. I found the towel you used in your attempt to clean up the pizza. You can start with the laundry and then do a deep cleaning in the kitchen."

Ethan set right to work. He hated household chores, but he was willing to do whatever he needed to make things right with his mom and sister. He worked right up until dinner despite his disappointment in not getting to work with the triplets for a while. Kolt wasn't home for dinner. Thank goodness. The last thing Ethan needed right now was Kolt getting more on his case. Ethan's mom took some soup to Harley who was still lying on the couch.

Just Ethan and his dad sat at the big round table. "I'm sorry about Harley, Dad. I think I may have a lying problem."

"Today was a pretty scary day. But I don't think Harley was in as much danger as your mom is letting on. She was just really scared. It would have been nice if you'd told us she cut her finger yesterday, though."

Ethan winced, "I didn't want you to think I wasn't responsible. And you guys seemed pretty busy with Aunt Jane."

His dad gave Ethan a half smile. "That is true. Maybe if we weren't so distracted with what my sister is going through, we would have noticed. But responsibility isn't covering our mistakes, Ethan. It's owning them. That's part of Aunt Jane's problem. She's got herself into a heap of trouble."

"What kind of trouble?" Ethan asked with a worried tone.

"Nothing you need to worry about. It's grown-up stuff."

Ethan mulled that thought over. He never liked it when his parents said something was grown-up stuff. It pretty much meant none-of-your-business.

His dad continued, "You know, we are all faced with decisions to lie or tell the truth every day. You've started a bad habit, but I believe you can break it. You just have to start with telling one truth at a time and refusing to lie. Once you see it can be done, it'll keep getting easier. Let's practice. Do you love pig liver for dinner?"

Ethan winced, "Ew! No!"

"How about cleaning toilets?"

"No," Ethan chuckled.

"Or watching Harley's television shows?"

"Definitely no!"

"Or skydiving from a plane?"

"NO!" Ethan gasped.

"See?" His dad winked before he took a big slurp of his soup. "You're already on your way to your new truth-telling self. Wish I'd tried that on my sister years ago." He muttered the last sentence mostly to himself.

* * *

Two Mondays went by before Ethan was allowed to coach the boys again. Every day after school, he was either at soccer practice or helping Harley with homework, keeping her entertained. He did everything his mom asked him to do, which was a lot! His parents were very preoccupied with whatever was going on with Aunt Jane.

Harley finished her antibiotics and became her usual cheerful self. John and Jack forgave Ethan and life felt almost normal again. Mr. Blair asked to move the triplets' coaching sessions to Wednesdays. Ethan arrived on the soccer field first on that third Wednesday. It was breezy, and leaves were blowing off the trees. Even still, he could hear the boys coming before turning to see them. They were squealing and jumping and kicking their soccer balls as they burst across the field.

"Race us, Ethan!" Ben challenged.

Beck jumped on Ethan's back.

Barton joined in as well, saying, "Down to the goal and back!"

Ethan smiled, remembering his first few soccer practices when he was just four years old. The thrill of the game still excited him. "Okay, you guys get started." He motioned toward the goal.

"No!" Beck argued. "We all start together."

"Okay, but look out...," Ethan teased.

"Ready-set-go!" Ben hollered so quickly it took Ethan a second to realize the three boys had already dashed off. He chased after them and easily caught up. Ethan realized he could beat them but hung back to make sure he didn't.

Ben touched the goalpost first. Beck and Barton ran right through. Ethan jogged up behind them. "Wow. You guys are fast!" Ethan complimented honestly.

Beck and Barton whooped and jumped up to chest-bump each other. Ben folded his arms across his chest and gave Ethan a scowl. He said in disgust, "You let us win."

Ethan was surprised by Ben's comment. "You don't really want to lose, do you?"

"I won't lose," Ben glowered.

"Okay," Ethan consented. He remembered the days when he thought he was unbeatable. He smiled inwardly and said, "On your mark..."

Ben set his feet to his imaginary start

line. Ethan lined himself up beside him.

"Get set!" Beck called from behind them.

"Go!" Barton yelled.

Ben shot off down the field with a speed Ethan admired. Ethan tore after him. They raced side by side until just in the last few feet, Ethan pulled ahead and touched the goalpost on the opposite end of the field. Ben reached out and touched it right after him. Beck and Barton came running down the field panting. "That was awesome!" they said.

"You got him, Ethan!"

Ethan turned to Ben expecting that scowl to grow, but instead Ben beamed from ear to ear. "Great race! Good job." Ben gulped between gasps of air.

Ben jumped up to give Ethan a high five. Ethan directed, "Now, let's get to work."

Ben focused even harder than that first week. Ethan could see new determination and an eagerness to please.

On the Wednesdays that followed, Ethan could see that the boys were improving. He felt good about his job. He made it a point to answer questions honestly. He almost quit worrying about Brick.

Then one Wednesday, Jeanie missed the bus and decided to stay and watch Ethan coach the boys. She sat at the end of the field on a bench with her notebook. Ethan remembered that she still thought he was doing it out of the goodness of his heart. What would she think when her dad came and paid him?

The boys' session went a little wacky that day because Ethan was so distracted. The strong wind also blew mini tornados of leaves around the field. The triplets kept chasing these leaf funnels.

Ethan kept glancing over at Jeanie. Sometimes she watched. Sometimes she wrote in her notebook. Sometimes she just stared up at the sky or watched the leaves swirling around the field. The last time Ethan looked over at her, he heard Beck yell, "Heads up!"

He looked back just in time to see a soccer ball headed right for his face. He couldn't get low enough to head-butt it out of the way, so he tried to catch it. He threw his arms up, but he was twisted at a funny angle. The ball caught his little finger with painful impact and bounced away toward Jeanie. The triplets came charging at Ethan yelling apologies. Jeanie scooped up the ball and ran over. The Blair children gathered around Ethan as he held his throbbing hand.

"Let me see it," Jeanie directed.

Ethan held his hand out. His smallest finger was bent at a nasty angle.

Ben shouted, "Wow!"

Beck cried, "I'm so sorry!"

Barton exclaimed, "You need a doctor!"

Jeanie went woozy and passed out.

Ethan forgot his pain as he tried to catch her with his good arm. He only succeeded in breaking her fall. The two hit the ground together.

Barton went into EMT superhero mode. Emergency medical technicians and ambulances were his passion. He knelt down beside Jeanie, grabbed her hand, and started yelling, "Jeanie! Jeanie, can you hear me? It's Barton. Wake up." He leaned his head down in front of her mouth to see if she was breathing.

Ethan thought Barton was about to

start mouth to mouth. Thankfully, Jeanie's eyes fluttered open. She looked around trying to figure out what happened. Then she realized she was on top of Ethan. "What happened?" She tried to get up.

"Just sit there, Jeanie," Barton said in his best first-grade doctor voice. "You shouldn't stand up right away after a fall."

Jeanie rolled her eyes at her brother. She was embarrassed to be sitting on Ethan. Ethan was embarrassed to have her on top of him. His finger still throbbed. The two of them untangled themselves and sat side by side unsure of what to do.

Barton took command. He stood up and pointed at his brother. "Beck, run into the school and tell them to call 9-1-1. Ben, go with him and get some ice."

Beck shot off toward the school before Jeanie could stop him. Thankfully, his dad's Jeep pulled up and Beck veered toward it instead. Ben chased after him yelling the situation to his dad as he ran.

Barton knelt on the ground by Ethan and Jeanie again. He held up his hand in front of Jeanie and said, "How many fingers am I holding up?"

"Two, goofball," Jeanie answered as she playfully pushed his hand down. "I'm fine."

Ben and Beck came running back with their dad in tow behind them. Barton stood and calmly explained the situation to Mr. Blair. "Dad," he began, "these two need medical attention."

Mr. Blair tried to keep a straight face. He crossed his arms, shifted his weight, and gave Barton a serious look. "I concur. How should we proceed, Dr. Blair?"

"Jeanie fainted and Ethan broke his finger. I suggest carrying Jeanie to the car. She needs hydration. We need to take Ethan to the hospital," Barton directed.

"I can walk." Jeanie stood and balanced herself. "I just can't look at Ethan's finger again. And where did you learn the word 'hydration'?"

Ethan looked at his now-pounding finger. He accepted Mr. Blair's offered help. With Ethan's good hand they linked wrists, and Mr. Blair hoisted him to a standing position. The group headed to the car. Barton insisted on holding Jeanie's arm. He directed Beck to take her other one. Jeanie looked over at Ethan as she walked between her brothers. She shook her head as if to say, "This is overkill but cute."

Mr. Blair called Ethan's mom and explained the situation. She asked him to meet her at the hospital since she was on that side of town. Ethan climbed in the front with Mr. Blair. Jeanie squeezed into the back with her brothers.

Once they all met up at the hospital, Mrs. McWyer checked in Ethan with the receptionist. Mr. Blair readied his kids to go home.

"Can't I stay, Daddy?" Barton begged. Ethan smiled inside that this kid was so interested in him.

"Sorry, kiddo. We need to get home to Mom's good cooking. Ethan is in good hands with his mom and the doctors."

The triplets each gave Ethan a hug and said good-bye.

Ben exclaimed, "I hope you get a bright blue cast! I'll sign it for you."

Ethan ruffled Ben's hair with his good

hand.

Beck just kept muttering, "I'm so sorry. I'm so sorry."

Ethan looked into his eyes and said, "Hey, accidents happen. This is nothing. I'll be fine. As long as it's not my ankle or foot, I'm good."

Barton's eyes drooped even lower as he said, "I wish I could stay."

Jeanie even gave Ethan a hug, which surprised him. She whispered, "I hope it feels better soon." Somehow, Ethan knew it would. He felt a warmth and comfort that he had not felt in a long time.

7 ~ Character Club

Ethan boasted a splint the next day at school. It wasn't a blue cast, but the foam was blue. Darren, Peter, Eddie, Brad, and several other boys gathered around once again for the story. Ethan realized what happened wasn't very exciting. When he saw Jeanie down the hall, he knew there was no point in trying to make up something. Plus, this was a chance for him to work on his honesty.

"I'm coaching Jeanie's brothers and one of them nailed me with the ball last night,"

Ethan reluctantly mumbled.

"That little punk. You shoulda just taken your good arm and punched him like the guy at the pool." Eddie put up his fists in a one-two motion.

"He's six, Eddie."

"Oh," Eddie said, lowering his eyes.

Jeanie joined the group. "How's your finger, Ethan?"

Ethan held it up for her to see the splint and said, "Six weeks with this thing. Boom."

Jeanie laughed. "Well, I'm glad it's not worse. Poor Beck cried himself to sleep last night. He felt so guilty for kicking that ball at you. He drew a picture for you."

Ethan felt sorry for the little guy. "Tell him not to worry. I've got a whole fan club thanks to him." Ethan motioned to the circle of boys surrounding him.

"No joke." Jeanie smiled. "That'll cheer him up. See you after school." She gave a little wave and continued down the hall where Claire waited.

"See you after school," Eddie mimicked in a high-pitched girly voice.

"Ethan and Jeanie...," Brad started to sing.

Ethan rolled his eyes and gave him a playful shove with his good arm. "Don't be a dork."

"Just be careful," Darren warned. "She'll write about you in her next book."

"It's nothing, guys. A bunch of us walk to Character Club together. Claire, John, and Jack all come too."

"Oh, Character Club," Eddie teased. "Maybe I should come so I can walk with Jeanie Blair too." He winked and elbowed Darren playfully. Darren looked away.

Ethan refused to be sucked into their banter. Besides, it was Claire he wanted to walk with. He simply replied, "You should. It's really fun. I never miss." Except for unexpected illnesses, that was a true statement. Ethan left the gang behind and headed into class.

* * *

As Jeanie, Claire, the twins, and Ethan walked to Mrs. Keller's, the sun shone warm and bright without a trace of wind. Ethan tried to chat with Claire, but she and Jeanie were deep in a gymnastics conversation. Ethan watched Jack collect trash again. He looked ahead down the road and saw a soda can in the gutter. "Race ya!" Ethan called as he ran for it.

Jack tore after him, but Ethan got there first. Ethan swiped the can up with his good hand and held it in front of Jack's face. "Who's rubbing off on who now?" He laughed.

Jack playfully threw the empty water bottle he just picked up at Ethan. Ethan jumped out of the way and ran toward the house. Jack scooped up the bottle again and chased after Ethan.

The boys dumped their trash in Mrs. Keller's recycle bins and washed their hands at her kitchen sink. The counters were lined with no-bake oatmeal-chocolate cookies. Ethan glanced at a little sign in front of them and quickly read, "TAKE SOME."

Ethan went to grab two, but Jack slapped his hand. "Ow! That was my bad finger!"

"Well, you deserve it. Read the sign."

Ethan looked again: TAKE ONE. "Oh,

I read that wrong." They each took one cookie and headed out to the backyard to grab water bottles from Mrs. Keller's cooler that she kept on the patio.

Jack scarfed down his cookie and joined the soccer game already in progress. Ethan sat on one of Mrs. Keller's red patio couches. He wanted to savor his cookie. Mrs. Keller usually only served super healthy snacks like cheese sticks and fruit slices. Besides, he figured he could use a break from soccer. He took a bite, leaned back, and basked in the late autumn sunshine.

Jeanie, Claire, and John finally came through the back door. John joined the soccer game, but the girls sat with Ethan.

"Why'd you guys take off like that?" Claire asked, then took a bite of her cookie.

"Just havin' fun saving the neighborhood." Ethan smiled and took a swig of his water. Claire turned to look at the game, and the sun caught her hair. Those curls! Ethan thought.

Mrs. Keller's son, Andrew, came out on the patio and called, "Hey everybody! We have a new guy joining us today."

Ethan choked on his water. He just knew he was about to see Brick walk through the door. He started coughing and sputtering.

Jeanie slapped him on the back several times and asked, "Are you okay?"

He was embarrassed now. He just nodded and bolted inside through another door into the bathroom. The water just went down the wrong pipe, but he couldn't stop coughing. The tickle in his throat kept setting off new spasms.

Ethan took deep, slow breaths hoping to calm his body down. Several minutes passed. He took some small sips from his water bottle. He looked at himself in the bathroom mirror. His face was all red and his eyes were watery.

Ethan closed the toilet lid and sat on it to focus better on his breathing. He took a few deeper breaths without a coughing spasm. The tickle in his throat was so annoying. He took another slow sip of water. Maybe he could head back out. He heard Mrs. Keller give the roundup call, so it was time anyway. What would he do if Brick joined Character Club?

He exited the bathroom and slowly headed back outside. There on the patio couch where he had been sitting by Jeanie sat . . . Darren!

A few of the older boys were introducing themselves. Ethan gave Darren a wave and a smile. Then he sat on Mrs. Keller's patio steps feeling the biggest relief he'd felt in months.

Mrs. Keller gathered the whole group close in and began, "Today is a new month, so we will begin studying a new character virtue. Our introduction game has been around a long time, but today I want it to demonstrate the importance of integrity. Can anybody tell me what that means?"

Everyone looked at Mrs. Keller with a blank stare. Clearly, no one had any idea.

"How about honesty?" she helped.

John called out, "Telling the truth."

"Not stealing," Wendy added.

"Yes, but it even goes deeper than that." Mrs. Keller encouraged more ideas.

Jeanie added, "Being true to yourself."

"Great ideas. Here is our definition." Mrs. Keller held up one of her posters that she kept for each virtue.

It said, *Integrity: Strength and firmness of character; keep your word, be completely honest and sincere.*

"To demonstrate how important strength of character is, today we are going to experience what happens when it is slowly chipped away."

Andrew and Karlie came out each carrying a tray. On each tray were several paper plates. Each plate sat under an upside down clear plastic cup that looked like it was full of flour. Ethan could tell there was something else in there on top of the flour but wasn't sure what it was.

Mrs. Keller explained that at the bottom of each cup, before it was filled with flour and flipped over, she had placed a dime. The dime represented each person's integrity.

"We will break up into groups of three or four. I'd like to mix you all up, so let's not have any all-girl or all-boy groups. Once settled, you will carefully remove the plastic cup and take turns slicing away at the flour with the plastic knife. As you make a cut, please share a time when you struggled with integrity or were tempted to be dishonest."

Ethan groaned inwardly. This was the very thing he'd been battling with since school started. This was not going to be an easy day. Mrs. Keller had a way of cutting straight to the heart of her students' issues. Sometimes he wondered if she spied on them at school or just really knew kids that well.

Mrs. Keller then put the fun spin she always puts on every activity. "If the dime collapses into the flour when you make your cut, then you need to fish it out using only your lips."

Andrew and Karlie tried to hide their grins, and several students laughed.

"This will be fun!" Jack announced.

Jeanie looked at Ethan, then Darren, and invited them, saying, "Join our group."

Ethan jumped at the chance to be in Claire's group. It seemed that Jeanie was the one who invited Darren, so Darren stayed close to her even though he knew most of the boys.

Karlie handed Jeanie a plate. Jeanie

carefully carried it to a spot in the grass that looked flat. Ethan, Darren, and Claire all sat in a circle around it. Jeanie pulled off the plastic cup. The flour kept the shape of the cup with the dime sitting on top.

"I'll go first," Jeanie volunteered. She picked up the knife. She paused, gripped the knife tighter, and then looked at Darren. "When I wanted to win that writing contest, I wanted it so badly that I made things up about people . . . including you, Darren. I'm sorry, once again." She made a small vertical cut near the outer edge of the flour tower. The dime remained sitting at the top.

She handed the knife to Claire who sat beside her. "I took candy from my sister's Halloween stash because mine was all gone. She caught me doing it and I told her I was borrowing it." Claire kept her eyes on the tower and made her slice. It kept standing.

"Borrowing?" Jeanie laughed. "I'd sure hate to get chewed candy back!"

Darren took the knife next. He turned it over in his hand like he was turning over his thoughts. Finally he began, "When my mom disappeared a few months ago, I didn't tell anyone. At first, I was embarrassed because we just didn't know what happened. People joked that she left us. That made me mad, but deep inside, I wondered if it was true. In a way, not speaking up was like lying to everyone. I blamed myself. If I had just talked to my dad about it, we could have worked through that waiting a lot easier." Darren paused. "And if I hadn't forgiven you, Jeanie, or the others who made up rumors, I'd be so much worse off now." He focused on making his cut. It went through clean and simple.

Jeanie looked at Darren and added, "I'm just so glad that she is getting better so quickly."

Ethan and Claire said in unison, "Me too." They locked eyes and grinned. Ethan glanced at Darren before taking the knife.

Once Ethan held the knife, several options he could share came to mind. He thought about all the different times he had been dishonest. He could tell them about Brick, which would definitely be the most awkward. He could share about the deception with the substitute or the snake. He could even share what he did to Harley. All of those felt really heavy at the moment. Then he looked at Jeanie and realized he lied like Darren by not filling her in on the whole story about working with her brothers.

"Jeanie." Ethan looked at her and gripped the knife. "I've let you think I'm volunteering to coach your brothers." He paused just a second to watch her face to see if she was following him. Then he finished, "But your dad pays me. It's like a job."

Jeanie looked down at the tower. "Oh," was all she said.

Ethan quickly made his cut. The once round tower now looked like a square. But the dime remained at the top.

A commotion behind them broke the silence in their group. Jack's cut had caused his dime to fall. Jack's whole group was either moaning or laughing. Jack dove into the flour without hesitation. He came right up with the dime between his lips. The rest of the group cheered for him. Jack's face was covered in white from his chin to his nose. He coughed and small puffs of white flour erupted from his mouth. His group roared with laughter.

Claire held out her hand to Ethan for the knife. "I'll go next." Claire could see Jeanie still blinking in a confused state over Ethan's confession.

"I was babysitting my little sister RyRy last month. We're not supposed to leave the house when we're home alone. It was a beautiful, sunny day and I wanted to go to the park. I convinced RyRy that it was okay to go and we walked over to play and hang out. I collapsed on the grass to watch the clouds roll by. I love to imagine what it would be like to ride on one of them." Claire stopped suddenly embarrassed that she might have revealed too much personal information.

Jeanie was dialed in. "Go on."

"I heard a cry and sat up. At first I couldn't find RyRy, but then I saw her under the swings. She fell off and skinned her knee. I carried her quickly home and washed her up as well as I could."

Ethan wished he had done the same for Harley. The guilt from not taking better care of

Harley welled up again inside him as he listened to Claire. Maybe he should tell that next. This actually did feel a bit freeing.

Claire continued, "But then I realized if my mom found out we'd been at the park, I'd be busted big-time. So I convinced RyRy to tell Mom it happened in our backyard. I made a liar out of my little sister." Claire's eyes were downcast as she began her cut.

Ethan felt a protective instinct toward Claire and announced, "I did the same thing to my sister. But I didn't clean her up and she got really sick."

Ethan's blurted admission startled Claire, and her knife cut went a bit askew. The dime tumbled down with the rest of the remaining tower. Claire and Jeanie gasped in unison.

Ethan felt responsible. "I'll fish it out. It was my fault. I scared you."

Claire laughed at him. "Not at all. I made the cut. I can do it." She pulled her hair back behind her with one hand and leaned down into the flour pile.

Darren laughed as she moved the

flour around with her nose. Jeanie giggled too. Ethan couldn't help but smile. It was hilarious to watch, and all those curls pulled back made him dizzy. A few kept escaping every time she moved. Ethan wondered what would happen when she let go. He desperately wanted to touch one.

Finally Claire came up with the dime, smiling with it between her lips. Claire dropped it into her hand. She let go of her hair, and the curls bounced back into her face sending the flour in every direction. The group all laughed. Jeanie wiped some flour off her jeans.

Ethan instinctively reached across the paper plate and pulled one of Claire's curls covered in flour. He stretched it all the way straight with his splinted hand and knocked the flour off with his good hand. Then he let go and watched it spring back.

Claire looked at him in shock. "Did you just pull my hair? Are we in kindergarten?"

Ethan suddenly realized what he did. "Uh. No. Sorry. I was getting the flour out." He paused as Claire smirked at him. "Although I've always wanted to see what your curls would do after being stretched all the way out." He was surprised how easily that admission came out.

Claire just guffawed at him sending more flour into the air. Then all four of them burst into uncontrolled laughter. Jeanie grabbed one of Claire's curls and repeated Ethan's gesture. Jeanie looked at him and said between giggles, "I do it all the time!"

By the time their laughter was under control, the other groups had all finished up. Mrs. Keller told everyone to head inside and get cleaned up if they needed to.

Claire and a few other girls headed for Mrs. Keller's bathroom where Ethan had his coughing spell earlier. Jack cleaned himself up by the kitchen sink along with Peter and an older boy named Lucas. They both must have made the dime's fateful cut in each of their groups.

Ethan sat on the floor in Mrs. Keller's living room with John and the rest of the lucky clubbers. Jeanie sat down and whispered in Ethan's ear, "I don't care that my dad pays you. You deserve it."

He looked at her and she smiled. Then she quickly moved to the other side of the room.

When everyone was neat and orderly again, they came and joined the group. Mrs. Keller asked, "Would anyone like to share their experiences from today's activity?"

Rachel, the girl Peter had thrown the worms on way back in September, spoke up. "I was with some girls at the mall last month, and two of them wanted us each to steal something. Maggie and I stood up to them and didn't do it. We went separate ways that night but later found out they got caught." Rachel winked at her best friend, Maggie, sitting by her side, and they squeezed hands.

Mrs. Keller smiled and said, "There's an old proverb that says, 'Whoever walks in integrity walks securely.' That is a great example! Thank you, Rachel."

Ethan rolled that saying over and over in his mind. Whoever walks in integrity walks securely. Whoever walks in integrity walks securely. It did feel good that Jeanie finally knew that her dad was paying him. Being dishonest with her hadn't felt good. Then he thought back to poor Harley. He sure didn't feel secure when his mom told him how sick Harley was from the infection. And poor Harley wasn't secure when she went to the hospital. Surprisingly no one in his group seemed to think he was a monster when he told them about it. Plus, Claire practically did the same thing!

But then Ethan remembered he didn't like his mom being mad at him, which reminded him of his lie about the field trip last month. He apologized, but had he changed? Ethan tried to focus on some of the things other kids were sharing. His thoughts kept turning inward, though.

When Character Club ended, the twins' mom picked them up for a dentist appointment, so Ethan walked home alone still churning over his thoughts.

He realized he hadn't been walking in integrity for a long time. It all started the first day of school because he couldn't admit how he got his black eye. It sure caused a lot of insecurity in him. All the bad dreams and fears of shadows chasing him frustrated him. Even today when he feared Brick might show up at Character Club! But was that a lie he wanted to make right?

Ethan mulled these thoughts over as he entered the house. He could hear his parents' voices coming from his dad's home office. Ethan didn't intend to eavesdrop, but when he heard Aunt Jane's name, he felt himself creeping closer to the closed door.

"But I don't want to help her," his mother's voice came through the door.

"I agree. She's frustrating. But when you tell this many lies over years and years, people just don't believe you anymore. No one will give her the benefit of the doubt in this situation. I don't even know if she knows when she's telling the truth or not," Ethan's dad answered.

"Well, it's no wonder she's got herself in this mess. She's not going to buy herself out of this one."

"I think if I can convince her to sell her house, we can help–"

"She is NOT moving in with us!" Ethan's mom interrupted. Ethan's eyebrows shot way up. He didn't want that either.

"No. No. Of course not. But maybe I can help her find a small apartment. She doesn't need all that space. It's the only way she'll get herself out of this hole."

Ethan heard some muffled tears, and then his dad asked his mother what was wrong. "I'm sorry to change the subject, but I'm worried about Ethan." Ethan's ears perked up as he heard his name.

"What? Why?" his dad asked.

"I'm afraid he's going to end up like your sister. He's starting down that path."

Ethan couldn't hear his dad say anything or see his reaction, but he backed away quickly down the hall. There was no way he would let himself turn out like Aunt Jane. He would figure out a way to come clean with his lies . . . and soon.

8 ~ Dinner Date

Ethan didn't even see a shadow of Brick that week. Ethan wasn't sure how to make an honest confession about Brick, but he knew at some point he would have to.

The weather changed and a heavy snowstorm blew through that weekend. It snowed all day Saturday and Sunday morning and left behind about ten inches. Ethan spent most of the weekend sledding in John and Jack's backyard. They built a mountain of snow at the top of the slope and slid down into the back fence. Sunday afternoon, they sledded for four hours nonstop until finally the twins' mom coaxed them inside with hot chocolate. She topped their cups with mini marshmallows and crushed candy canes.

The storm wasn't enough to close school the next day. The temperature stayed cold, though, so the snow didn't melt. Ethan's soccer practices were canceled all week and so was his time with the triplets on Wednesday.

Finally by Thursday, the sun shone brightly and the temperature slowly began to rise. The regular crew trudged to Mrs. Keller's house through the sloppy inches of snow that were finally beginning to melt. Jeanie and Claire held on to each other's arms in their big heavy coats to keep from slipping. Ethan and the twins ran and slid wherever there was enough slush to loosen their traction.

When they arrived, several towels lay inside the front door where everyone piled their boots and shoes. The kids hung out in the kitchen, dining room, or back room that led out to the yard. Maneuvering through the crowd to get to the snacks was a little trickier than normal with so many people in the kitchen. Ethan managed to grab some pretzels and a cheese stick. He headed with the twins into the family room to sit on the floor to eat. Darren also sat on the floor leaning up against the fireplace mantle. Ethan was glad Darren came back to club again.

Mrs. Keller started a little earlier than usual since there wasn't much to do inside. She took them all downstairs to her basement where she had arranged enough chairs for everyone to sit in a circle. Ethan sat between the twins and Peter. Jeanie and Claire sat on Peter's other side. Then Mrs. Keller introduced what she called an Integrity Game.

Mrs. Keller made a statement. If the statement was true about you, you were supposed to move to the right or left however many seats she directed. If someone was still sitting in that chair, you just sat in their lap. She started simple, "If you are wearing white socks, move right one seat."

John jumped up and sat on top of Jack who wore blue socks. Jack protested, "Hey! You don't have to sit so hard!" Everyone laughed. Ethan's socks were gray, so he stayed put. However, several other kids got up and moved. Peter moved to sit on Ethan. Jeanie sat in Peter's empty spot.

Now there were a few empty seats around the circle. Mrs. Keller continued, "Move clockwise one seat for every sibling you have."

John and Jack got up and moved together over a seat. Thankfully the girl next to them had a sibling and got out of the way before they both plopped down on her! Peter hopped up and moved two seats. Ethan moved with him and sat on top of Peter this time. Then Ethan watched Jeanie point as she counted, "One, two, three." Her finger ended pointing right at him. She laughed and plopped down on top of Ethan who was on top of Peter. She giggled, "This is like an Ethan sandwich!"

"My legs are gonna fall asleep," Peter protested from the bottom of the pile.

The game continued. Sometimes Mrs. Keller told them to move clockwise, sometimes counterclockwise. Sometimes she told them to move one seat, sometimes two. Sometimes it depended on how many they owned of something, like pets.

Everyone was laughing and out of breath as she kept giving funny directions. After several minutes went by she changed the nature of her statements.

"Move one seat counterclockwise if you've ever stayed up after your parents told you to go to sleep." Most everyone kind of chuckled and moved a seat. A few kids stayed in place.

"Move one seat counterclockwise if you ever cheated on a test." The room got quiet. A few kids hesitated before they moved.

Mrs. Keller gave one last statement. "Move one seat counterclockwise if you've ever thought you were better than someone else who made a mistake." Nervous glances cast around the room. Finally, Rachel stood and moved a seat. Maggie moved right behind her. It seemed to cause a ripple effect, and one by one every student moved over a seat.

Mrs. Keller smiled and nodded, "I'm very proud of all of you. It's not always easy to admit when we've made a mistake. It takes integrity to own up to it. You all just took an important step toward integrity today. Let's move upstairs." She herded them all back up the stairs for the lesson.

Ethan felt good that he took a step toward integrity. Maybe he wouldn't turn out like Aunt Jane after all.

Once they were all seated in her family room, Mrs. Keller explained, "That game was a way for you to practice integrity. Most of the questions were easy, but when they got harder, did you struggle?"

Mrs. Keller watched as several students nodded their heads. Then she continued, "Who are some people you know or have read about who show integrity or are known for their integrity?"

"George Washington! He chopped down the cherry tree and then couldn't lie about it," Peter called out.

"Mother Teresa. She's a saint," Maria mentioned.

"Abraham Lincoln," Wendy called out at the same time Jack added, "Martin Luther King, Jr."

"My dad," Jeanie added. "He's the most honest man I know!"

Mrs. Keller continued, "Having integrity is staying true to who you are no matter who you are with. Martin Luther King, Jr. fought for change, but he did it peacefully. He stayed true to peace and eventually paid the ultimate price for it. Now we have a day every year when we remember his sacrifice."

Mrs. Keller continued by sharing something about the integrity of each person the kids had mentioned. When she mentioned Jeanie's dad, she shared how important it is to have role models we know and see often to inspire us and keep us accountable to the truth.

Ethan's mind wandered. He remembered the story Mr. Blair told him on the field trip bus. Then he thought about how his dad told him that his mother overplayed Harley's infection, and he was always telling them that they would talk about things in the summer that they never again talked about. That didn't seem very honest. And then there was Aunt Jane. Maybe he didn't have the best role models in honesty.

Mrs. Keller continued, "Integrity is also about doing the right thing even when no one else is watching. Remember our definition: *Integrity: strength and firmness of character; keep your word, be completely honest and sincere.*

"There's another old proverb that says, 'The fear of human opinion disables.' When you are so worried about what other people think of you that you don't speak up for yourself, it makes it impossible for you to accomplish what you hope for."

Mrs. Keller used this comment as a transition to announce the next service project. "Unfortunately, over at the new sledding hill, there have been a lot of people littering all over. So next week, we will take a field trip over there and our service will be to clean it up. Bring all of your winter gear, including gloves. We will spend however long it takes to clean up that hill."

A few boys eyed each other, but no one said a word. No one ever complained about Mrs. Keller's ideas. She always transformed something that didn't sound very exciting into something wonderful. Ethan and Jack challenged each other silently with their eyes. It sounded like they would have some more opportunities to out-clean each other in their community.

Mrs. Keller continued, smiling that mischievous smile that kept the kids always guessing. "When we finish, we can enjoy some time sledding ourselves."

There it was. The kids all cheered. More snow was on its way this weekend, so the hill would be primed and ready. Ethan and the twins slushed home excited to tell their parents about the service project and the sledding opportunity.

That night at dinner, Kolt told his parents he would like to bring his girlfriend over Friday night. Ethan's mom was ecstatic. She began pulling out recipes almost on the spot.

Friday night came and John ended up at Ethan's house too. Jack needed to go back to the dentist for a filling, so Ethan's family kept John for dinner. Ethan's mom put a leaf in their round table to make it more oval for the two extra guests.

Kolt seemed nervous. He wore his best jeans, a long-sleeved, button-down shirt, and a matching tie. Kolt paced back and forth in front of the window. Ethan thought Kolt looked ridiculous. He never planned to dress up for a girl, not even Claire! Harley watched out the window with Kolt.

As a car finally pulled up, Kolt raced out the front door. He met his date as she stepped out of her little blue Volkswagen bug. Harley squealed, "Punch buggie!" She ran across the room to where Ethan and John were playing a game and hit Ethan in the arm.

"Hey!" Ethan whined. "We only play that in the car!"

John laughed and punched Ethan's other arm. John's hit was definitely harder, and Ethan rubbed it with his splinted hand.

Kolt brought his girlfriend in and introduced the family to Alyson. She wore stylish jeans with fancy boots that Harley went crazy over. Kolt took her coat. Her dark hair hung in long, loose curls over her shoulders. They weren't the kind that would go "boing" like Claire's, but Ethan thought they were pretty enough. She wore a studded birthstone nose piercing with matching stones in her second holes. Her first piercings boasted long, thin chains that came to her chin.

Ethan was impressed that his parents didn't get weird over Alyson. They didn't start eyeing each other and reminiscing about how they met. As they all settled in at the table, Ethan's parents started asking polite, but boring questions.

Ethan and John tried to sit still and simply eat, but every once in a while one would kick the other under the table setting off a foot war. Harley, on the other hand, was dialed in to every word. Her eyes shone with wonder.

As Ethan's mom passed her famous meatloaf, Ethan's dad asked about Alyson's family.

Alyson answered, "Well, it's really just my mom, me, and Ashley."

"OOOOh! You have a sister! Maybe she can be my friend!" Harley gushed.

"Oh no." Alyson smiled politely. "Ashley is my brother."

John spit out his mashed potatoes in

surprise. Ethan forgot his manners as he and John fell into uncontrollable snickers.

Through chuckling tears, Ethan managed to ask, "How'd he get that name?"

John added with a cackle, "Was it his fairy godmother?" The boys collapsed onto each other into howling fits.

Ethan's parents just sat there not moving, probably overcome with their younger son's lapse in civility. His dad's eyes were as big as saucers, not knowing how to handle the situation. Ethan's mother's fork was literally frozen in place in front of her mouth until she dropped it and scolded, "Ethan!"

Kolt glared at Ethan. Alyson looked nervously around the table at each parent and each boy. Finally, she swallowed and answered politely during a lapse in the laughter, "It was my father's name. He died right before my brother was born. My mom gave him that name to remember and honor my dad."

The chortles abruptly stopped, and the boys said in unison, "Oh." Ethan's eyes went to his lap. He heard his mother clear her throat.

Ethan looked up at her and could

read her mind through her facial expression. He looked at Alyson and said solemnly, "I'm sorry." He looked back at his mother who was still urging him to say more. So he added, "That was really rude of me. I hope you can forgive me."

John cleared his throat and said, "Me too."

Kolt shook his head in disgust and grabbed Alyson's hand and gave it a squeeze. An awkward silence followed. Ethan wondered what it would be like to grow up without a dad. Then he realized Kolt didn't have a mom when he was little. Ethan wondered if that's what bonded Kolt and Alyson.

Then Harley saved the dinner conversation by saying, "Can somebody pass the corna-ma-cob? I'm starving!"

Ethan's mom chuckled and corrected as she passed the plate, "That's corn on the cob, Harley."

Then Harley asked, "Why are some people born with a sparkle in their nose?"

Alyson blushed but managed a giggle. She leaned in toward the table as she thought up an answer quickly. She whispered quietly to Harley but everyone could hear, "Because I have a secret. Deep down inside, I'm a real princess!"

Harley's eyes widened in admiration. Everyone laughed and dinner was saved.

John's mom picked him up after dessert. Ethan's parents sent Ethan and Harley downstairs so they could spend some adult time getting to know Alyson better.

9 ~ Facing Fear

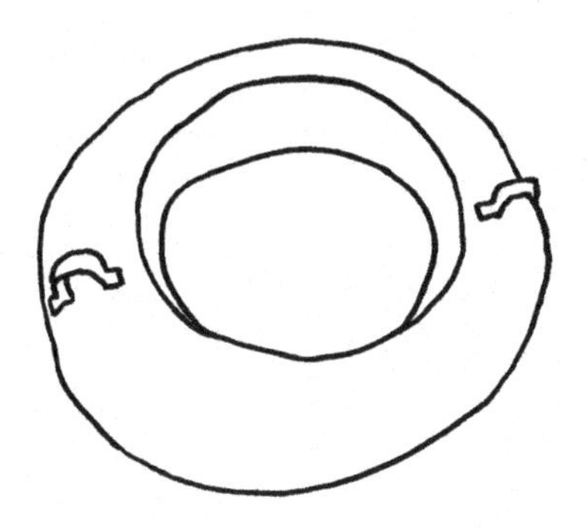

The day of the service project arrived. Fresh snow fell each day leading up to Thursday. Ethan felt antsy after missing so many soccer practices. Several parents' cars were lined up in front of Mrs. Keller's house again, including Ethan's mom's and Jeanie's dad's.

Ethan, John, Jack, and Peter all rode with Mrs. McWyer. The boys talked nonstop about who would pick up the most trash and who would race down the hill the fastest. Ethan was super excited. He had never gone sledding anywhere but in John and Jack's backyard. Ethan couldn't wait to sled on a real hill–after everyone picked up all the trash, of course.

Ethan's mother pulled her car up to the parking lot in front of the hill. Ethan's eyes widened in horror. He'd never seen a hill so huge. It looked like it rose straight up to the sky. He gulped as the other boys scrambled out of the car whooping and hollering. All his pent-up energy dissipated.

Mrs. Keller handed out garbage bags as she instructed, "Now remember, it's not a race or a contest. Just leave no piece behind. Work together and then we can enjoy some time sledding. Don't forget to look for slightly buried trash either. Fresh snow may have covered some."

Ethan collected his bag. His hands inside his gloves were clammy with sweat. He turned slowly toward a tree where he saw some trash. He lifted his boots haltingly through the snow. He watched John and Jack jump over snow piles and race toward some empty cans scattered around. Ethan knew everyone would collect their trash as quickly as possible to get to the sledding hill. But he was in no hurry. His biggest fear reared its ugly head as he felt threatened by the hill looming behind him. He walked as if his boots were made of lead.

No matter how slowly Ethan moved, the others finished the job. Before he knew it, Mrs. Keller was calling everyone. He trudged over with his almost-empty trash bag. John and Jack held a bulging bag between them. Peter and Darren dragged a heavy one across the snow. Even Jeanie and Claire did pretty well with the bag they shared.

"Great job, ladies and gentlemen," Mrs. Keller exclaimed. "Let's load these into the back of my car and get sledding!"

The kids cheered. Jeanie's dad insisted on putting half of the trash bags in his Jeep. Once the bags were all loaded, Peter yelled, "Come on, Ethan! Let's go!"

Peter ran over to the edge of the hill where the pile of tubes sat. There were saucers and even a few old-fashioned sleds in the pile. The parents brought everything they owned, so it seemed. Peter grabbed a tube and started trekking up the side of the slope. John, Jack, and the other boys bolted after him. Ethan knew he couldn't sit this out at the bottom. He and the other boys bragged all the way here how fast they would go and who would race whom. He plodded over to the pile and pulled off a tube. Ethan slowly stumbled up what felt like a mountain, dragging his tube along with him.

When Ethan reached the top, Peter and the twins sat in their tubes ready for launch. "Let's go!" Peter called out.

A few other boys jumped on their tubes and sailed immediately away. Ethan looked down the hill from the top. It appeared even more intimidating from up here. His mind flashed to the basketball game he attended with his dad. Fear gripped his heart. His stomach turned a belly flop.

"You guys go without me. I'll be down in a second." Ethan gulped down his lie. He had no intention of following them down this monster hill. So much for his new honest self.

"See ya!" Peter called and pushed off. The rest of the boys went right after him, except Jack. They bellowed and shouted the whole way down. Ethan stood holding his tube by his side. He watched them each safely come to a stop at the bottom before he realized that he wasn't alone.

"I'll wait for you, Ethan." Jack smiled sitting in his tube next to Ethan.

"No. I'm not ready. Just go."

Jack just sat there.

"Look, I'm not ready. I'll get you guys on the next round."

Jack still sat there staring hard at Ethan.

"What?" Ethan questioned with frustration.

Jack looked up at Ethan from his tube. Jeanie and Claire plopped their tubes down on the other side of Jack. "What are you guys waiting for?" They grabbed hands and went sailing down the hill together, screaming as they went.

"You'd think something was chasing them the way they're screaming," Jack commented. "Have a seat."

Ethan dropped his tube and sat in its center. The cliff felt like it could reach out and strangle him. He felt his stomach lurching. Jack studied Ethan. "You can do this, man."

Ethan looked over at Jack. "Of course. I just need a minute." Ethan watched Peter and the other boys collect their tubes at the bottom. They looked like ants as they started back up the hillside.

"A minute isn't going to help. I know you're scared, but–"

Ethan cut him off. "I'm not scared. I'm just not ready." Ethan remembered the last day of summer sitting on top of the tube slide. Now he was sitting on a tube with the same problem. Except this wasn't a simple sister dare. This was full-on peer pressure.

"Ethan!" Jack's sharp call snapped him back to the present. "I've known you since kindergarten. I know you're afraid of heights. You just have to admit it and let people help you."

"No way . . . That's not it. I'm just not ready. I need to adjust my gloves."

Jack glared at Ethan and crossed his arms in front of his body. If Ethan wasn't so scared, he would have laughed. Jack looked ridiculous sitting in that tube with his legs sticking up above his folded arms trying to look angry.

The rest of the boys finally reached the top and lined themselves up with Ethan and Jack. "Are we ready now?" Peter prodded.

"I'm not sure I feel like sledding today." Ethan answered. "It's too cold." He started to climb out of his tube.

"What?!" Peter gasped. "Did you say it's too cold for sledding as you're at the top of the hill ready to go?"

"Yeah. Not feelin' it today, guys."

"Will you just cut the lies and show some integrity?" Jack urged with an edge of frustration.

"Huh?" Peter clearly was clueless.

Ethan looked at Jack, then John, then Peter. Mrs. Keller's whole lesson came flooding back into Ethan's memory in an instant. The tower of flour. The integrity game. Then his mom's voice flashed in his head: I'm afraid he's going to end up like your sister. Ethan collapsed into his tube. He wanted to be true to himself. He wanted to have his friends trust him. He was tired of feeling completely disabled. He wanted to be a person of integrity. Ethan finally admitted, "I'm afraid of heights, guys."

"Thank you!" Jack threw his hands and feet up in the air. He looked like a bug stuck on its back trying to cheer.

Peter still looked confused. John smiled and slapped Ethan on the back. "I was nervous the first time too. This is a big hill. But we can all go together. That's what friends are for."

Peter jumped on his tube, finally getting it. "Come on, Ethan. It's more fun together anyway."

Ethan looked down the hill and gulped. He saw Mrs. Keller and his mom talking at the bottom of the hill. Mr. Blair stood with them. He thought he saw Kolt's car pulling into the parking lot. Finally he muttered, "Okay. Let's do this."

Jack grabbed Ethan's tube and Ethan grabbed his. Peter grabbed the other side and John hooked onto Peter's. They all started scooching their tubes toward the edge until gravity took over.

Ethan wanted to scream. The first five seconds he thought his stomach was going to fly out of his throat. Ethan's tube lurched forward and picked up speed. Ethan imagined himself back in the tube of the waterslide. But this time the thrill of the speed at which he soared down the mountain took over. It helped that he could see where he was going.

Ethan lost his grip on the other boys' tubes. But he realized he was okay! Ethan imagined he was flying across the soccer field, light as air. The wind in his face blew his hair back. When he finally slid to a stop at the bottom, he felt elated. The other boys coasted to a stop next to him. Everyone seemed to pause waiting for Ethan's judgment.

Ethan yelled, "Again!"

The boys all cheered and gathered up their tubes with Ethan. They raced back up the hill. Ethan didn't notice the huge smile of pride on his mother's face. She was beaming. Mrs. Keller gave her a big hug.

By the third trip down, Ethan no longer even hesitated at the top. He just jumped on the tube and slid right down. The next time he came to a stop at the bottom, Ethan slid right to a stop at the feet of Kolt who was holding

Harley's hand. Ethan looked up at them and noticed Alyson standing behind them. Right next to her was the face of a boy Ethan would never forget. The face of his nightmares and fears. Brick.

Alyson motioned toward Brick, "Hi again, Ethan. Kolt wanted me to introduce you to my brother, Ashley."

Ethan froze. It took him a second to realize that Ashley was Brick's real name. Ethan watched recognition come over Brick as well. Brick remembered Ethan. Ethan gulped and stood up. He looked into the face of his haunting shadow of the last several months.

Ashley scowled. "That's Brick to you."

Kolt grinned his devilish grin. "You guys remember each other?" Ethan wondered how long Kolt knew his girlfriend's younger brother was his tormenter from the pool. And how long had Harley known?

Peter and the other boys gathered round. Brick stood with his legs wide apart and folded his arms across his chest. His eyes narrowed as he snarled, "Ridin' the tubes today? Is it easier without water?"

Alyson looked a little surprised at her brother's remark. Ethan's eyes widened, and he hoped his friends wouldn't figure out who this was. Peter, after warming up his brain at the top of the hill, was thinking more quickly now. "Dude! Is this the guy you decked at the pool? Is he dissin' you now? Let's all take him down!" Peter stepped forward pounding his fist into his other hand.

Ethan knew the lying needed to stop. This was the time to come clean and make the change Ethan wanted to make. Ethan also realized that Brick was caught in as much a lie as he was. Brick was pretending to be this tough kid because he wanted to cover up that his name could be for a girl.

Ethan knew what he had to do. His friends had just helped him conquer his fear of heights. Hopefully they could forgive him for this lie too. It was time to confess all. He put his arm in front of Peter to stop him. He looked at Harley standing with Kolt. Ethan chose to be a good example to her, like Jeanie's dad had been to his little brother.

Ethan explained slowly, "It didn't really

go down like that, guys." He motioned toward Brick. "Brick pushed me down the slide. I hit my eye on the edge of the tube. He knocked me underwater at the bottom, but I never even touched him besides that. Harley jumped on him and kneed him in the face."

"What?" Peter exclaimed. "You mean all this time we thought you were sticking up for your kid sister and she was sticking up for you? That's messed up."

"I know. I'm sorry, guys. I lied. I've been kinda stuck in a bunch of lies. But I want to be done. It's been so hard hiding from Brick and trying to keep the story straight. That's why I'm owning up to it with you all." Ethan turned to Brick. "Brick, I'm sorry I lied about what happened with you. I know it didn't really affect you, but I still shouldn't have done it."

Ethan immediately felt like a ton of bricks came toppling off his shoulders. He didn't realize how heavy lies can get until he let them go. He wanted to do a cartwheel or something. He felt so free.

Brick softened at Ethan's confession. He thought about Ethan's words for a few seconds, then shrugged. "I guess I actually lied too. No way I was telling my friends some little girl gave me that fat lip."

Harley put her hands on her hips behind Brick and started to make her pout position. Ethan grinned at her, then added to Brick, "It sure feels good not to have that hanging over my head. I'm glad you get it." Ethan looked around at the group of boys. John and Jack were smiling big smiles at him.

Peter looked a bit miffed but scratched his head and said, "I guess that's cool."

Finally Harley's patience ran out, and she asked in a frustrated tone, "Can we stop all this talking and just sled?"

Ethan grinned and agreed. "Sure thing, sis."

Ethan grabbed Harley's hand. Then he heard Jack from behind him introduce himself and say to Brick, "Would you want to sled with us?"

Brick shrugged again and answered, "Sure." Brick followed the other boys to the side of the hill and grabbed a tube.

Ethan stood frozen in place. Was that it?

Was Brick one of the guys now? All that angst and now they were just going to sled together like they'd been friends forever? He listened to the others introduce themselves as they walked away.

Harley sensed his hesitation and looked up at him. "Kolt talked to me on the way to meet Ashley today. He said the best way to get rid of an enemy is to make him your friend. And that's what he planned to do with the two of you."

Ethan looked back at her and asked, "So you're okay with Brick? I mean Ashley?"

Harley smiled her biggest smile, "Yep. Now let's go sled! Come on, Kolt. You too!" She yanked on Kolt's hand to pull him toward the tubes.

Kolt squeezed Harley's gloved hand and gave her a wink. Kolt let go and playfully punched Ethan in the arm as he walked by. "You're all right, kid."

Ethan's grin spread from ear to ear. He beamed with pride at his brother's praise. Ethan grabbed a tube for himself and one for Harley.

When Ethan reached the top, he threw down the tubes. He flopped on his and yelled, "Come on, Harley! Race you to the bottom!"

Discussion Questions

Teachers: For advanced discussions, projects, and more ideas to connect other subjects to this book, visit our website at **www.characterclubonline.com**

1 ~ So Long, Summer

A) What are some things you are afraid of? Why?

B) Who is someone you look up to and try to impress? Why?

C) How do you think Ethan should have handled the first day of school with his black eye?

2 ~ First Day Flub

A) What first day of school traditions do you have in your home?

B) How do you think Ethan feels about lying to his mom?

C) What do you think Brick told his friends

about the pool incident?

3 ~ Shrewd Substitute

A) How would you behave if you had Mrs. Murray for a substitute teacher?

B) Why do you think Ethan lied to Mrs. Murray?

C) What do you think will happen when Mrs. Murray finds out Ethan left class early or that there wasn't really a mouse?

4 ~ Field Trip Follies

A) Describe a fun field trip you have been on or would like to go on.

B) What are some pros and cons of having cell phones on field trips?

C) Why do you think Mr. Blair told Ethan the story about his brother and the bowling alley?

5 ~ Good Game?

A) Why do you think Kolt was so angry at

Ethan for lying to their mom?

B) Why do you think Ethan didn't play well at the evening game?

C) How do you feel about the offside play that Ethan learned so well but Kolt was disturbed by?

6 ~ Triplet Trouble

A) How do you think Ethan should have dealt with Harley's cut?

B) Why do you think having Jeanie at the triplets' coaching session made Ethan so nervous?

C) What do you think made Ethan feel better about his situation at the end of the chapter?

7 ~ Character Club

A) Why do you think Ethan choked when he heard there was a new boy at club?

B) How would you define integrity?

C) What does this phrase mean to you:

"Whoever walks in integrity walks securely"?

8 ~ Dinner Date

A) How do you think you would respond to some of Mrs. Keller's more difficult questions?

B) What do you do (or what can you do next time) when the right thing is hard (or unpopular) to do?

C) Discuss what you think each family member was thinking after Ethan and John insulted Alyson's brother's name.

9 ~ Facing Fear

A) Why do you think Ethan was moving so slowly during the trash cleanup?

B) What steps can you take to overcome some of your fears?

C) What are some examples of how Ethan's journey in this book helped him toward Integrity?

Glossary

Antics *noun* - foolish, outrageous, or amusing behavior.

Basked *verb* - to lie in or be exposed to a pleasant warmth.

Caricature *noun* - a picture, description, etc. ludicrously exaggerating the peculiarities of a person.

Circulation *noun* - the continuous movement of blood through the heart and blood vessels.

Civility *noun* - courtesy; politeness.

Coaxed *verb* - to attempt to influence by gentle persuasion.

Deferred *adjective* - postponed or delayed.

Embellish *verb* - to enhance (a statement or narrative) with fictitious additions.

Guffaw *verb* - to laugh loudly and boisterously.

Indifference *noun* - lack of interest or concern.

Intimidate *verb* - to make timid; fill with fear.

Melancholy *adjective* - soberly thoughtful; pensive.

Methodical *adjective* - painstaking, especially slow and careful; deliberate.

Placate *verb* - to soothe, pacify.

Predicament *noun* - an unpleasantly difficult, perplexing, or dangerous situation.

Ruckus *noun* - a noisy commotion.

Saunter *verb* - to walk with a leisurely gait; stroll.

Technician *noun* - a person who is trained or skilled in the technicalities of a subject.

Vertical *adjective* - being in a position or direction perpendicular to the plane of the horizon; upright; plumb.

Want to read more about Ethan, Darren, Claire, Jeanie, and all the other Character Club kids? Then join Jeanie on her journey toward compassion in "Jeanie Blair, Author Extraordinaire."

Made in the USA
Columbia, SC
06 February 2018